Carol Ericson is a bestselling, award-winning author of more than forty books. She has an eerie fascination for true-crime stories, a love of film noir and a weakness for reality TV, all of which fuel her imagination to create her own tales of murder, mayhem and mystery. To find out more about Carol and her current projects, please visit her website at www.carolericson.com, "where romance flirts with danger."

Her Alibi

CAROL ERICSON

MILLS & BOON

First published in Great Britain 2019
by Mills & Boon, an imprint of HarperCollins*Publishers*
1 London Bridge Street, London, SE1 9GF

Large Print edition 2019

© 2019 Carol Ericson

ISBN: 978-0-263-08383-5

MIX
Paper from
responsible sources
FSC
www.fsc.org   **FSC® C007454**

This book is produced from independently certified
FSC™ paper to ensure responsible forest management. For
more information visit www.harpercollins.co.uk/green.

Printed and bound in Great Britain
by CPI Group (UK) Ltd, Croydon, CR0 4YY

Chapter One

The sea crashed on the rocks, and the tide tried to drag her back under but she resisted its pull. She forced open one eye, the lid weighted like a manhole cover.

To keep it open, she focused her dry eyeball on the filmy white curtain billowing into the room from the French door ajar to the balcony. Another wave from the ocean below made its presence heard as it broke and then clawed at the rocky shore. She could almost taste the salt from the sea spray on her tongue.

She licked her lips. The air in the room lay heavy upon her, and she still hadn't managed to open her other eye. She lifted a lethargic arm and rubbed her closed eye, hoping to stimulate it.

She blinked against the stinging sensation and rubbed again, smearing moisture across her cheek to her ear. Had she been crying in her sleep? That deep, dark slumber she couldn't seem to shake?

Raising her hand in front of her face, she wrinkled her nose. Not tears, blood. She hadn't had a bloody nose since she was a kid. She pinched the bridge of her nose with two fingers, sniffing, and her nostrils flared at the tinny smell that seemed to invade every pore.

The odor revived her, stunning her like a prod. She jerked her bare limbs beneath the silk sheets. She bolted to a sitting position, the back of her head hitting the headboard. Pain, all out of proportion to the tap of her skull against the wood, coursed through her body, and she gagged.

As if that bump had awakened every nerve ending in her body, her right hand began to throb. She spread out her fingers, the red cuts on her hand standing in stark relief against the white sheets.

What the hell happened? Why was she bleeding, and why was she naked in her ex-husband's bedroom?

She scrambled from the bed, tripping over something soft on the floor in the semidarkness. Gasping, she fumbled for the light switch on the wall next to the bed and jabbed at it with her thumb.

Her gaze dropped to the floor, and she staggered back, her mouth agape. A scream gathered in her lungs but lodged in her chest, choking her instead. Closing her eyes, she drew in a deep breath. Somewhere deep down inside, she knew vomiting would only make this situation, whatever it was, much, much worse.

Her self-preservation, one of her strongest instincts, took control of her brain and her eyelids flew open. She extended her leg and with her big toe, she prodded the shoulder of her ex-husband, crumpled on the floor.

Her investigatory digit met cold flesh, and

the reality rushed in on her, just as surely as those waves were rushing to shore outside that window. She clapped a hand over her mouth and hissed through her fingers, "Niles?"

The *s* hung in the air and only the drapes floating into the room whispered a response.

She fell to her knees and crawled toward Niles's still form. Covering two fingers with the bedspread that hung to the floor, she placed them against his neck. The once-vibrant man, who couldn't seem to sit still for a second, didn't have one ounce of life left in his body.

She sat back on her heels and surveyed the opulent bedroom she'd painstakingly decorated a lifetime ago. What had happened in this room?

She dug a knuckle into her temple. She couldn't remember coming into the bedroom with Niles last night. She'd come back to the house with him in his car after the drink they'd shared at the Marina Sports Bar. He had the file she'd wanted to see in his home office.

He did so much work from home she didn't figure it for a ploy. Niles didn't need ploys. He'd moved on to another woman shortly after their separation. Hell, who was she kidding? He'd moved on to multiple women *before* the separation.

Then what? Had he drugged her? She ran her tongue around her dry mouth. Had he not wanted to show her the file?

She peered at her hands and the cuts on her right palm. Her gaze darted to the bloody wounds gouging Niles's back. He'd been stabbed…to death.

They'd fought last night. They always fought. That was why they'd got divorced. Civilized people divorced. They didn't kill. She hated Niles, but she never wished him dead.

The breeze filtering in from the open door tickled her ear. She shook her head. Not just dead. Murdered. And she'd blacked out… again.

Adrenaline coursed through her veins, and she sprang to her feet. Her head swiveled back and forth, her gaze tripping over her clothes in the corner. Why had she taken them off? She dragged in a deep breath. If she panicked now, she'd get herself into even deeper trouble.

Get dressed. Get out.

As she tiptoed to the jumble of clothing, a building dread accompanied each step. There could be only one reason for her to strip off her clothes: if they were soaked with blood. She leaned forward, pinching the material of her blouse between two fingers and pulling it free from the pile.

The spotless white silk had her releasing a noisy breath. She grabbed a handful of the black slacks and shook them out—dry as a bone. As dry as her mouth.

Her underwear had been dislodged from her slacks and fell back to the floor. She scooped up her bra and panties and put them on over her cold, clammy flesh. Had she showered at some point last night?

She pressed her nose against the skin of her upper arm—not sweaty, but not exactly fresh, either. She crept into the bathroom and nudged the light switch with the side of her hand, casting a warm glow over the gray tiles with their bright blue accents.

No droplets of water appeared on the floor of the walk-in shower. No damp towels littered the bathroom or hung on the racks. She edged up to the vanity and peered at her reflection in the mirror.

A pair of wide violet eyes stared back at her, and a smear of blood created a line from the corner of her eye to her ear. That was her own blood from the cuts on her right hand. She didn't have a speck of Niles's blood on her. She stuck two fingers in her mouth and then rubbed the red streak from her face.

If her clothes weren't bloody and she hadn't taken a shower, surely she'd be covered in his blood if…? But she'd blacked out.

She spun away from the mirror and scanned every corner of the bathroom. Nothing looked out of place—except her standing here in her underwear.

She whipped a hand towel from the rack and wiped the light switch, and the sink and shower faucets for good measure. Then she rushed back into the bedroom and erased her fingerprints from the light switch in there, too. She didn't have to wipe down the entire house, as she'd been here recently. Hell, she used to live here.

She inspected the bed, squinting at the pillow and sheets, searching for strands of her dark hair and blood from her cuts. Those would be damning, but she couldn't afford to spread even more of her DNA around by going into the laundry room and washing the bedding.

Then she crouched beside Niles's dead body and studied the cuts on his back and the ripped, slightly freckled flesh. She shivered.

She looked at her hand, the thin red lines of the cuts creating a horizontal pattern on her palm. She reached up and buried her fingertips in her hair, tracing over a tender lump on the back of her head. Had she and Niles had some kind of fight? A physical altercation? Could his killing have been in self-defense?

She bunched up her hand into a fist and pressed it against her stomach. Self-defense when she stood to gain 100 percent control of Snap App? Self-defense when everyone knew they had been fighting over the company for months?

Nobody would believe her—not with her past. She couldn't afford to be at another scene involving a dead body.

She picked up the towel and continued wiping down surfaces in the bedroom. With a brisk nod, she dropped the towel to the floor and picked up her slacks next to it.

She slipped into the black pants and gasped, patting the pockets. Her lashes fluttered as she huffed out a breath. She'd left her phone at home last night on the charger. Her battery had been dying lately and she couldn't be happier about it now. She didn't need her cell phone signal pinging in this house at this time.

She pulled her blouse over her head. As she reached for the top button, she grabbed threads instead. Her button had popped off— the oversize multicolored, highly unique button.

With her head pounding, she dropped to her knees and ran her hands across the wood floor and underneath the dresser. Her fingers stumbled across the button and she slid it across the floor and dropped it into the pocket of her slacks. Then she stepped into the high heels placed next to each in perfect alignment.

She scooped up the towel and gave the room a final look over her shoulder from the bedroom door. She froze. *The knife.*

What if the knife had her prints on it? Her head swiveled from side to side. What knife? She hadn't seen a knife anywhere.

Her gaze slid to Niles's body. He had stab wounds on his back, but what about his front? If she rolled him over, she could leave more evidence of her presence here. If she didn't, she could be leaving a murder weapon with her prints on it.

She kicked off her heels and approached Niles. She feared him now more than she ever had alive. Still gripping the hand towel, she pushed at his inert form enough to tilt it on its side. Before he fell back to the floor, she'd determined there was no knife beneath him—nothing beneath him except more blood. This had been angry overkill.

It hadn't been her anger that had killed him. But then she'd blacked out.

She grabbed her shoes in one hand and shuffled out of the room backward, as if she expected Niles to jump up and point an accusing finger at her, and then turned and jogged down the curved staircase, sweeping the towel along the banister for good measure. She and Niles had come back to the house for some file, and she still had every intention of leaving with that file.

She scurried into Niles's home office and scanned the clean surface of the mahogany desk. She and Niles hadn't even made it far enough to get the file. But she knew exactly where they were.

With the towel still clutched in her hand, she dropped her shoes and crouched before the desk drawers, pulling open the bottom one. She shoved the hanging files aside and then snatched a letter opener from a pencil holder on the desk. She jammed the point into a circular release at the bottom of the drawer and slid open the false bottom.

She released a sigh. The labels indicated the file folder she wanted was on top of some other folders and a few other items. Niles must've got it ready for her. She removed the folder, replaced the false bottom, closed the drawer and wiped down everything.

Gripping the folder in one hand, she turned away from the desk and tripped to a stop when she saw two crystal tumblers on the counter of the wet bar. She yanked the towel from where she had it draped over her shoulder, rinsed out both glasses, wiped them down and put them back on the shelf behind the bar.

The computer had to be her next stop, to check the footage from the security cameras. Covering the mouse with a tissue from Niles's desk, she navigated through the security software.

She drew in a quick breath as her mouth dropped open when she realized the system had been disabled. Had Niles done that earlier? Had his killer? Had she?

Now she needed to sneak out of here…and find herself an alibi.

CONNOR DUG HIS feet into the sand and squinted at the surfers battling the heavy surf—and each other.

He pulled out his video camera, zoomed in and started filming the Cove Boys and their antics in the water. Summer might've ended but the rowdy group of surfers who ruled the cove with a belligerent localism never stopped when they thought outsiders were riding their waves.

Connor caught the Cove Boys dropping in on others' waves, cutting them off, yelling and making rude gestures. This footage would help with the lawsuit.

The Cove Boys' aggressive behavior had its desired effect as, one by one, the harassed surfers came to shore in defeat.

A couple approached him, their boards under their arms. The man reached back and yanked down the zipper of his wetsuit. "Are they always like that?"

"Yep." Connor held up his video camera. "But we're trying to stop it. Some local surfers who don't like the reputation of the cove are bringing a class action lawsuit against these guys—and I just captured some solid evidence."

"Good. It's about time someone did something about these guys."

Out of the corner of his eye, Connor saw a surfer clambering from the surf and coming at him. He turned, widening his stance on the wet sand, his muscles tense.

Jimmy Takata, one of the Cove Boys, threw

down his board. "What's up, Wells? What's the camera for?"

"Whaddya think? You guys can't stop even when your attorney tells you to lie low."

Jimmy lunged at him, and Connor dropped the camera on top of his bag and raised his hands. "You wanna go there?"

"You're playing with fire, Wells." Jimmy leveled a finger at him. "Your old man doesn't rule this town anymore, and he did a crap job when he did."

Connor's eye twitched behind his sunglasses. "Aren't you kinda old to be playing beach bully, Jimmy?"

"Never too old to protect your own. Besides, you're not a cop anymore, so stop trying to recapture your glory days." Jimmy guffawed as he scooped up his board and waded back into the water.

Connor crouched and stashed the camera in his bag. Then he hitched it over his shoulder and scuffed his bare feet through the dry sand to the line of cars on the road above the beach.

He slid behind the wheel of his truck and tossed the bag on the seat next to him. Gripping the steering wheel, he let out a breath. If he could help break the stranglehold the Cove Boys had over the best surfing spot in San Juan Beach, it might go a little way toward restoring the town's former luster.

It seemed a million years ago since his father patrolled this small beach community as its police chief and the residents could trust each other and trust authority. Then the drugs moved in and all that ended—along with his father's life.

Connor swallowed the bitterness that flooded his mouth and took a swig of the warm water from the bottle in his cup holder. He'd leave this place, as others had, if it weren't for the land and his father's dream. Didn't he owe that to him?

Someone rapped on his window and he jumped. He peered through the glass at the couple from the beach and powered down his window.

The guy stuck his hand into the open space. "Thanks, man."

"For what?" Connor jerked his thumb toward the beach. "They're still out there intimidating people."

"Yeah, but if that lawsuit prevails and those idiots are slapped with an injunction, they're going to think twice about their localism—and your video footage should help."

The woman held out a business card. "If the attorney needs witnesses, give me a call. We'd be happy to help."

"Thanks." Connor plucked the card from between the woman's fingers. "I'll give this to the lawyer filing the lawsuit."

With a wave of his hand, Connor cranked on his engine and pulled away from the gravelly shoulder, spitting dust and sand in his wake. After a few miles, he made a turn to the east, away from the coast and the town of San Juan Beach.

The narrow, two-lane road wound into the low-lying hills and the early-fall temperature rose several degrees as he escaped the sea breeze. The hotter the better. His grapevines needed the warmth.

On the way to the house, Connor pulled over and jumped out of the truck. He cupped a bunch of grapes in his palm and sniffed—the sweet had started to overpower the tart—right on time, even though this crop wouldn't be the harvest for the wine. He had to wait another year for that.

Good thing he was a patient man.

As he made the last turn, he hunched over the steering wheel and squinted at the white car in his driveway. Someone had ignored the no-solicitors sign posted at the entrance to his property—probably another one of those Realtors. That shiny cream-white Lexus looked exactly like a Realtor's car.

His jaw hardened, and he threw the truck into Park. He pushed out of his vehicle at the same time a woman emerged from the Lexus.

As she floated toward him, her hands held out, Connor blinked. Her perfume wafted toward him and enveloped him in her spell.

When she reached him, she wrapped her arms around his waist and rested her head against his shoulder, her chestnut hair lifting in the breeze, his capture complete.

Her warm breath caressed the side of his neck as she whispered in a husky tone, "I'm in trouble, Connor. And I need an alibi."

Chapter Two

Connor's body, still hard and strong, stiffened. She knew he wouldn't be putty in her hands, but she'd hoped she wouldn't have to bring out the big guns.

He stepped back, and she unwound her arms from around his waist. She didn't want to be clingy.

Narrowing his blue eyes, he folded his arms across his unyielding chest. "What now?"

She gazed over his shoulder at the empty road bordered by grapevines and pasted a smile on her face. "The vineyard looks good. I can't wait for the first bottle."

He snorted, "Are you really trying to butter me up? You should know better."

"I need to ease into this." She squeezed his rock-solid biceps. "Can we talk inside?"

"Hang on."

He turned back toward his truck, opened the door and ducked inside, giving her a spectacular view of his backside in his board shorts. From the look and feel of Connor's muscles, she wouldn't be surprised if he worked this vineyard single-handedly, but he must still be spending time at the beach, given his sandy bare feet and the burnished-gold sheen on his brown hair.

He walked toward her, a black bag slung over his shoulder. As he passed her, he nodded toward the house. "Follow me."

"Hardly the red carpet I was expecting after all this time."

"Maybe it's more than you deserve after all this time."

She sucked her bottom lip between her teeth. She definitely needed the big guns this time around.

As she walked into the house she expelled a soft sigh. "You redecorated."

"This is my house now, not my parents'. What's wrong? You don't like it?"

She ran a hand along the back of the cream-colored leather sofa, which had replaced an overstuffed floral one that had been littered with his mother's handmade pillows. "It's an improvement."

He placed the bag on a granite island that separated the kitchen from the living room, where a wall once stood that had supported a shelf showing off Connor's surfing trophies.

"Do you want something to drink? No wine…yet."

"As much as I could use some alcohol right now, it's still morning and I need my wits about me…all my wits." Or at least the ones she still possessed after last night's blackout.

"I have water, orange juice and iced tea from a bottle."

"Tea, please." She perched on the edge of the sofa, the soft leather almost sighing beneath her weight, and wedged her purse next to her feet.

When Connor exited the kitchen holding

two glasses, the ice clinking with each of his steps, she patted the cushion next to her.

He handed her the glass, tossed a coaster onto the coffee table hand carved from a log and took the chair across from her.

Looked like he wanted to keep his wits about him, too. The two of them had always shared a magnetic attraction to each other, but maybe he'd been able to shut down that magnet after their last contact a few years ago.

"Tell me what's going on." He took a long gulp of tea. "Is it that husband of yours?"

"Ex-husband."

"Right. You're still fighting with him about that multimillion-dollar company?"

"It's much worse than that, Connor."

"Just spill it, Savannah."

"Niles is dead…murdered."

Connor's eyebrows shot up to that lock of brown hair that curled over one eye. "Murdered? Wouldn't that be all over the news? I know I'm kind of a recluse these days, but I do have a TV—cable and everything." He jabbed a finger at the huge flat screen that claimed the space above his fireplace.

"It's… He's… I don't think he's been discovered yet."

Connor jumped from the chair, and the tea splashed over the side of the glass clutched in his hand. "What are you telling me?"

"I found him. At his house. Dead."

"And you didn't call 911?"

"Of course not."

"Of course not?" He threw his arm out to the side. "No, why would anyone call the police upon discovering a dead body, especially the dead body of your ex?"

"Exactly." She took a small sip of tea and avoided his wild-eyed stare.

He stopped pacing and landed in front of the couch, looming over her with iced tea dripping from his hand onto the polished hardwood floor. "What the hell happened to him, Savannah? Why didn't you call the police?"

She shook her glass to rattle the ice. "He

was stabbed to death, and I didn't call because the police would've arrested me."

"Why?"

"Because I woke up in his house, in his bed, and I don't remember how I got there." She closed her eyes and held her breath.

The shocked stillness reverberating off Connor in waves made her more nervous than the agitated pacing. She peeled open one eye and swallowed.

A muscle throbbed at the corner of his mouth, and the fingers curling around the sweating glass sported white knuckles. His blue eyes had darkened to the color of a stormy sea.

Then he blinked, drained the tea in one gulp, wiped his palm on the leg of his board shorts and set the glass on the coffee table. "You'd better start from the beginning."

Warm relief flooded her body and she almost collapsed against the sofa cushions. This was the Connor she'd hoped to see—in control and even-keeled. He hadn't agreed to anything yet, but he hadn't thrown her out on her derriere, either.

Sitting up, she squared her shoulders. "Niles and I met for a drink last night to discuss some business. I had come across something in the books and wanted to see some files."

"Why didn't he just send over the file? Why the meeting, the drink?"

She studied his square jaw, clenched in disapproval. Did she detect jealousy in that question?

"Niles had been wanting to discuss other aspects of the business with me for weeks and figured this was his opportunity to have me at his mercy." She cleared her throat. "I really wanted those files, so I agreed."

"How did the meeting go?"

She ran her fingers through her hair, avoiding the sore spot on the back of her head. "Like all our meetings. We ended up in an argument."

His eyes flickered, but he took a seat on the edge of the coffee table and she eked out a little sigh because he was no longer looming over her.

"Did anyone at the bar notice you arguing?"

"I'm sure a few people did. We exchanged sharp words and may have got a little loud, but there was no knock-down-drag-out."

He rubbed his knuckles across his clean-shaven chin. He'd shaved off the beard since the last time she'd seen him. Bearded or not, the man still pushed all the right buttons in all the right places.

She licked her lips, and his gaze bounced to her mouth and then back to her eyes.

"What happened next? How'd you end up at his house? That house in La Jolla, right?"

"Yeah, that one." She caught a drop of moisture on the outside of the glass with her finger and touched it to her temple. "Niles had left the file I wanted at the house. I had to go with him to retrieve them."

"Go with him? You didn't drive your own car?" He tipped his head at the window, toward the Lexus in his driveway.

"I walked to the bar. It was close to my house and you know I don't like to drive after even one drink."

"Is that what you had? One drink?"

"Two." She held up two fingers in a peace sign and then brought the fingers together. "Scout's honor."

Unless she'd downed whatever was in that crystal tumbler at the house.

"I'm not checking on you, Savannah. I believe you. What I'm trying to get at is if you were drunk when you left the bar with him."

"Absolutely not. I don't get drunk…anymore."

"So why'd you black out? Do you remember going to his house? Driving in the car with him?"

"I do remember getting into his car. I remember more arguing on the way to the house, arriving at the house and then…" She shrugged. "Nothing after that. I don't remember what we did at the house. I don't know how I lost my clothes and ended up in his bed. And I sure as hell don't know how he wound up dead."

"And you didn't…"

"What?" She jerked her head in his direction.

He swiped a hand across his mouth as if to keep the words from tumbling out. "You're telling me that someone broke into Niles's house, murdered him in a violent manner and you were allowed to sleep peacefully through it all. Why weren't you killed along with Niles?"

"That, I can't tell you." She skewered him with a gaze. "You almost sound disappointed."

Connor pushed up from the coffee table and stalked to the kitchen. "Don't play the poor-me card. I know you too well."

He thought he did, but she'd kept secrets from him before.

He buried his head in the fridge and popped up with a bottle of beer in his hand. "I'm not offering. Someone needs a clear head here, but it's not gonna be me."

"Beer for breakfast?" She held up her hands to deflect his scowl. "Never mind. And I already told you, I have no idea why the killer left me undisturbed…almost undisturbed."

"Almost?" He took a swig of beer and hunched over the kitchen island.

She jabbed her index finger into her chest. "I did not voluntarily take off my clothes for Niles, and I did not crawl into his bed."

"The murderer took the time to strip you naked and place you in Niles's bed? Where was Niles's body?"

"On the floor next to the bed."

"Next to you?"

"On the floor."

He snapped his fingers. "Did you check the security cameras? A place like that, a guy like that—he had to have video surveillance."

"All disabled."

He scratched his chin in an absentminded manner. He must've just lost the beard and missed it, although why Connor's facial hair occupied her thoughts at this crucial moment was a mystery. She squeezed her thighs together and huffed out a breath. No, it wasn't, no mystery.

"Murder weapon?"

"Gone."

"Blood?"

"All over Niles and the floor beneath him, but only a little on me and none on my clothes."

"You had blood spatter on you?"

"I wouldn't call it spatter." She curled her right hand into a fist. She didn't want to show him her palm, but she couldn't hide it. He'd notice it anyway.

Holding her hand out to him and spreading her fingers, she said, "The blood came from some cuts on my hand."

He sucked in a sharp breath, and then skirted the counter and charged toward her. She shrank back when he dropped to his knees in front of her and took her wrist between his fingers.

But she had nothing to fear from Connor.

With a gentle touch, he traced a fingertip over each cut, sending chills down her spine.

"These aren't very deep…and they're on the wrong hand."

"The wrong hand?"

"The wrong hand for stabbing. You're left-handed."

She clasped his shoulder with her left hand. "I knew there was a good reason to run to you. D-do you think someone's trying to set me up for Niles's murder? Because I do. That's what I think."

"Could be. Do you have a motive?" He dropped her wrist and rose to his feet, as her hand slid from his shoulder.

She rolled her eyes. "Take your pick. We were fighting over the business. With his death, I get the whole thing, controlling interest back in my lap. A-and there's something else."

He had returned to his beer and raised his eyebrows as he took a sip.

"Life insurance." She knotted her fingers in front of her. "Lots of life insurance."

"It's natural to assume a spouse would be the beneficiary of life insurance, even after a divorce. It's not necessarily the first thing most people going through a separation think about."

"Niles Wedgewood is not most people. He *did* think about dropping me as his beneficiary after the divorce in favor of his new girlfriend, Tiffany, and his junkie twin brother, Newland, and his sister, Melanie, up in San Francisco, but I convinced him we should leave each other as our beneficiaries until we had the business worked out."

"And people know this?" Connor tugged on his earlobe, a sure sign of worry.

"His divorce attorney knows it."

"How much are we talking?"

She dropped her chin to her chest. "Millions."

"With Niles's death, you stand to get the business and millions of dollars in life insurance money."

His gaze sharpened and his eyes looked like chips of ice, sending a flutter of fear to

her belly. She'd better get used to that look—
especially if she couldn't produce an alibi
for last night.

"Looks bad, huh?"

He nodded. "Did it occur to you for one
second to call the police?"

"You know more than anyone why I won't
do that. No, it never occurred to me. I need
an alibi, Connor. I need you."

"You want me to lie to the police for you.
Claim you were here last night."

She leaned forward, planting her hands
on her knees. "Mom and I lied for your father."

There it was.

Connor's eye twitched at the corner.
"There's no footage of you at the house. You
didn't drive your car, so it wasn't parked in
the neighborhood. How'd you get home?
Taxi? App car?"

"Do you think I'm stupid?" She sprang up
from the couch, excitement and hope fizzing through her blood. He was going to help

her. "I walked, and if you think that was easy with heels on, it wasn't."

"You walked home, got your car and drove straight down here?"

"I showered and changed first, but I didn't waste much time."

He snapped his fingers. "Cell phone? The police are going to pull your records. They're going to know your phone was at Niles's house last night at precisely the time he was murdered."

"I didn't have my phone with me."

His head jerked back. "You didn't have your phone? Who doesn't carry their cell with them?"

"My battery has been dying on me. I left it at home, charging. I thought I'd be walking up to the bar to meet Niles for a quick drink, a discussion and those files."

"And then you drove down here with it turned on? They're gonna see that, too."

"Foiled again." She held up one finger. "I turned the phone off when I plucked it off the charger. It's off even now."

His eyebrows formed a V over his slightly sunburned nose as he pinned her with a slitted gaze before turning away from her.

The look sent a chill up her spine. Despite her explanation, he was wondering why she hadn't brought her phone with her to the bar...but he'd see she'd been telling the truth about her phone.

"If the police don't believe you...or me, they can track your license plate. There are cameras on the highway between here and La Jolla. If they want to, all they have to do is enter your license plate number and—" he flicked his index finger against his thumb "—they could get a hit, placing your car on its way to San Juan Beach today instead of last night."

"I removed my plates."

Connor swung around, his longish hair brushing his shoulders. "You could've been pulled over for not having plates."

"I figured it was worth the risk for just the reason you mentioned. Did you think I wasn't listening to you all those times you went on and on about police work and new innovations?" She tapped the side of her head. "It fascinated me. I was listening."

"What's your story?" He folded his arms, ready to listen.

"I was upset after meeting with Niles. I made him drop me off near my house, and then I hopped in my car and came down here to see you." She strolled to the window and rested her forehead against the glass. "I was here at the time he was getting stabbed."

"Why would you rush to my place? We haven't seen each other in four years, not since your marriage."

"We were…in love. Everyone in San Juan Beach knows that. I never got you out of my system. Never forgot you. Never stopped wanting you back." Her breath fogged the window, and she drew a line through the condensation.

The silence yawned between them until she couldn't take it anymore. She did a slow turn and met his eyes. "Is that…believable?"

"I suppose it could fool *some* people." The

frost dripping from every word made it clear she hadn't fooled him. "But we're gonna have to make it stick."

"How? What do you mean?"

"You can't go running back to your former lover and then leave him a few days later to get back to managing your multimillion-dollar company and spending Niles's life insurance money."

"I could if my lover rejected my advances."

"He wouldn't do that."

"He wouldn't?"

"You wouldn't have turned to him in your hour of need if you didn't think you'd meet fertile ground. If I'm going to lie for you, you're going to have to see this through. You're going to have to stick around for a while to give this story legs."

"I can do that—if you'll have me."

He leveled a finger at her. "I'm not going to get caught in this lie. I'm not going down for you—no matter what you and your mother did for my dad."

"I understand. It's in my best interest that we don't get outed—life or death, actually."

"Did you pack a bag or rush to me with just the clothes on your back?"

"Of course I packed a bag. It's in my trunk."

"I'll get it." He held up one hand. "Keys."

She grabbed her purse from the floor by the sofa and dragged her keys from a side pocket. She tossed her key ring to him, and he caught it with his outstretched hand.

"Be right back."

She watched him for a few seconds out the window and then turned, her lips twitching into a smile. It had been time to play her ace in the hole, but she knew she could get Connor to come around to her way of thinking. Even though he'd been a cop once upon a time, he had no regard for the police anymore. No trust in authority. Not much trust in her.

She sauntered toward the hallway and peeked into the first bedroom, the master suite, which Connor had transformed with dark woods and rich jewel tones. She didn't know he had such good taste—unless he'd had help.

She'd come to San Juan Beach with confidence that Connor didn't have a woman in his life. She still had her spies in this town, and they kept tabs on Connor for her. It wasn't exactly stalking—just a healthy interest in the one man she'd love forever, but could never have.

The front door slammed and Connor yelled out her name, as if she weren't down the hall.

She tripped back toward the living room and poked her head around the corner. "What's the commotion?"

"What the hell is this?" He waved a plastic grocery bag above his head.

"I don't know what you have there." She wrinkled her nose as she eyed the bag.

He yanked on the handles, pulling it open. "You don't know what this is?"

Her heart pounding against her rib cage, she crossed the room on shaky legs.

Connor thrust the open bag under her nose,

and she staggered back…away from the sight of the bloody knife.

"Savannah, tell me the truth. Did you kill your ex?"

Chapter Three

Connor studied Savannah's face as she peered into the plastic bag at the bloody knife.

Her big violet eyes widened, and her lips parted. Those eyes, a color he'd never seen before in his life, and the long lashes that framed them gave Savannah a look of innocence—but he knew better.

Who thought to leave a cell phone at home and remove a car's license plates without something to hide?

Savannah's bottom lip quivered as she dragged her gaze from the bloody evidence in front of her to his face. "I—I don't... No!"

She spun away from him, clutching her belly. "I didn't put that in my car. You found it in my trunk?"

"I found it in the spare tire well."

"Why were you looking in there?" She glanced at him over her shoulder, her mouth tight as if she blamed him for the presence of the knife.

The knots in his gut tightened. He wanted to trust Savannah, believe her crazy story. God, he loved this woman…once.

"The corner of the cover wasn't lying flat, so I lifted it. The bag looked out of place. What's it doing there, Savannah? Is it the murder weapon?"

"How do I know?" She lifted her shoulders to her ears and turned to face him. "I'm telling you, Connor, I blacked out when I got to Niles's place."

"The point being, you could've got into an argument with him, continued your argument from the bar even and…"

"Stabbed him multiple times in the back?" She shook her head back and forth.

"Maybe it was self-defense." He tied the handles of the bag together and placed it on the floor by the front door—not that he could leave it there. "Maybe the fight got physical, and he attacked you with a knife. You got it away from him and struck back."

"That's insane, Connor. I didn't have any…" She stopped and touched the back of her head with her fingertips.

"Any what? What's wrong?"

"I have a bump on my head. I was going to say I didn't have any injuries, but I have this lump on the back of my skull and these cuts on my hand."

His feet had been rooted to the floor ever since he'd entered with the knife and a terrible dread in his gut. Now a new urgency propelled him forward.

He took Savannah by the shoulders. "Turn around."

She presented her back to him, and a silky fall of dark hair rippled across her shoulders.

He nestled his fingers in the strands of her hair and slid them up to her scalp.

She winced and sucked in a sharp breath.

"Here?" He traced a large, hard knot on Savannah's head.

"Ouch. That's the spot."

"You didn't have that before you woke up this morning?"

"No. I don't think the skin is broken, and I didn't notice any blood in my hair."

"He could've pushed you, and you fell back against something."

"Maybe that's why I blacked out. Oh, Connor." Dipping her head, she pressed a hand to her forehead. "I don't know what happened last night."

His hands dropped to her shoulders again and he massaged his thumbs between her shoulder blades. "We're going to figure it out, Savannah."

"And what if we figure out I'm responsible for Niles's death?"

He turned her around to face him and kissed her forehead. "We'll deal with it."

"And what about that?" She pointed a slightly trembling finger at the bag by the door.

"We should get it tested for blood and fingerprints."

She jerked back from him. "Are you crazy?"

"I thought you wanted to find out who killed Niles." He folded his arms and dug his fingers into his biceps to keep from touching Savannah again. That never seemed to end well for him.

"Yes, but how are we going to ID blood and prints from the knife without taking it to the police?" She sliced a hand through the air. "I'm not doing that, Connor."

"I think I can work around that."

"Connections?"

"Maybe a few." His father *had* been police chief in this town for over twenty years, before the sheriff's department took over and swallowed up the San Juan Beach PD. "In the meantime…"

"In the meantime, get rid of it."

"I'll find a place." He aimed his foot at the suitcase he'd dragged in with the knife. "Why don't you unpack and get ready for our first appearance?"

"Our first appearance where?" She twisted a lock of hair around her finger.

"In public. If you showed up on my door-step last night, we'd be out and about by now...or at least we should be to prove you're here."

"Makes sense." She tossed her wound-up hair over her shoulder. "Are you sure you want to do this?"

"Like you pointed out earlier, I owe you for what you and your mom did for my dad. You never let me repay you for that."

"Because even though Mom and I lied... and said Chief Wells killed my stepfather in self-defense, it still led to your dad's death."

Connor gritted his teeth. "Self-defense or not, it would've ended for Dad that way. Your stepfather's associates were not going to let anyone get away with killing Manny Edmonds without payback."

"My mom was always grateful for...what your father did."

"My dad would've done anything for your mom." Apparently it ran in the Wellses' blood to do anything for the Martell women. Dad's devotion to Savannah's mother had broken up his marriage to Mom and ended his life. And Connor's own devotion to Savannah had strained his relationship with his mother. How would this latest association end?

"Brunch?"

"What?" Connor ran a hand down the side of his face.

"I'm going to change while you get rid of that knife. Are we having brunch or lunch out to show my presence in San Juan Beach?"

Savannah sure seemed anxious to dispose of what was probably the murder weapon. "I'm not going to dump it."

"Okay, whatever." She strode past him and grabbed the handle of her suitcase, yanking it up. "I don't want to know what you do with it."

"Shouldn't we take a look on TV or the computer to see if Niles's body has been found yet?"

She held up one hand in front of her face. "I don't want to know that, either. Better to feign surprise when the cops come calling."

With a toss of her head, she tipped back her bag and dragged it across the floor to the hallway.

As she veered toward the guest room on the right, he called out, "Master suite. We're back together, remember?"

Without a word or backward glance, she changed course and wheeled her bag into his bedroom.

He bent over and snatched up the plastic grocery bag by one handle. As it dangled from his fingertips, he stared at the spot where Savannah had disappeared into his bedroom.

He'd wanted Savannah back in his life for so long and now she was here in the flesh—needing him, sharing his bedroom, willing to engage in a pretend romance with him.

Turning, he grabbed the front door handle. How could this possibly go wrong?

SAVANNAH SMOOTHED HER hands across the cotton skirt that hit her midthigh. How many more ways could she feel guilty for dragging Connor into her mess?

Mom had dragged Connor's father into her messes, and here she was, carrying on the famous Martell tradition. She and Mom had lied about the night her stepfather was shot and killed, all right, but it wasn't for the benefit of Chief Wells.

Savannah could never tell Connor the truth about that night; he would never look at her the same way again. He'd blame her for his father's death. And because she had to keep this secret from him, they could never have a relationship—not a real one.

When she heard the front door open, she grabbed her purse from Connor's bed, and swung it by her side as she marched into the living room. "Ready?"

He spread his arms wide and his gray T-shirt stretched across his chiseled chest. "As long as it's casual."

"Is there anything but casual in San Juan Beach?"

"You haven't been here for a while. A couple nice places popped up along the strand, still casual dress, though."

The cell phone that had been charging on Connor's kitchen counter dinged, indicating a new text message. She swallowed. "I'd better see who that is."

Connor nodded.

She slid the phone across the smooth granite surface and tapped the incoming message. The words on the screen screamed at her. She read them aloud for Connor's benefit. "'Have you heard? Call me.'"

"Who's it from?"

"It's from Dee Dee Rodriguez. She's Niles's admin assistant at the office."

"You'd better call her."

"So it starts." She went to her contacts and called Dee Dee's number.

Dee Dee didn't even wait for the first ring to end. "Savannah, have you heard about Niles?"

"No. What happened? What's wrong?"

"He's dead."

"What are you talking about?" She lifted

her eyebrows at Connor. Did she sound convincing? She put the phone on speaker, so he could hear everything, steer her in the right direction.

"Niles is dead, Savannah. Murdered."

"Murdered? Is this a joke, Dee? It's not funny." *Feign disbelief.*

Connor nodded.

"Would I joke about someone's murder?"

"I—I don't believe you. Why haven't I heard anything?"

"I just found out. The police are here." She lowered her voice. "They were asking about you."

Savannah licked her lips, her gaze darting to Connor's face. "What happened, Dee? Who found him? I was just with him last night."

"All I know is that his housekeeper found him this morning. I don't know how he died. If…if you saw him last night, it must've happened after that, or this morning before the housekeeper arrived."

"Oh, my God. This is terrible. I—I'm

going to turn on the news or look it up on my computer."

"I'm not sure the news is out there yet. Where are you, Savannah? I'm sure the police are gonna head to your place."

"Probably, although Tiffany is closer to Niles than I am now—in every way, including physically. I'm not even in San Diego. I went south to San Juan Beach."

"Oh, my God. Are you with that hottie from the picture you showed me?"

Heat clawed up Savannah's chest and she turned away from Connor. "Yeah, I'm down here with Connor."

"Lucky girl, unlucky Niles. Stay safe. Maybe there's some kind of hit out on both of you."

Savannah chewed her bottom lip. If that had been the case, she'd be dead, too. "I will. If the cops ask you about me again, you can tell them I'm in San Juan and would be happy to talk with them."

"I will. It's gonna be crazy at the office."

"I can't imagine anyone's going to get any

work done, so why don't you all just take the rest of the day off?"

"Well, we can't just… Oh, right. You're the boss now, aren't you?"

"Tell everyone there to take a mental health day."

"Will do."

Savannah ended the call and spun around. "How did I sound?"

"Convincing. Now, get on your laptop like you said you would."

She dropped her purse on the floor where she stood and returned to the bedroom. She pulled her laptop from a zippered pouch on the side of her suitcase and brought it into the kitchen.

As Connor hovered over her shoulder, she powered on the computer and did a search for Niles Wedgewood. Her hand trembled as she clicked on the first link that popped up. "Local news outlet already has the story, but no specifics."

Connor leaned in closer, his warm breath stirring her hair. "Just a snippet—body believed to be that of Niles Wedgewood, co-founder and CEO of Snap App, discovered in his ocean-side mansion in La Jolla. No further details at this time."

"The police are going to call me, aren't they?"

"Homicide detectives. They'll probably want to interview you face-to-face, especially once they find out you were the last person to see him alive."

"I'll be ready." She snapped down the lid of her laptop and rubbed her hands together. "Now, let's go eat and make my presence known in SJB."

Savannah bounced along in the passenger seat of Connor's truck as he pulled onto the road from the property he'd inherited from his father. She rolled down the window and inhaled the scent of the air sweetened by grapevines.

"I think I can detect the aroma of wine already."

"This time next year, I hope to have my first harvest."

She tapped on the window. "I didn't notice a name for the winery. Have you thought of one yet?"

"I suppose the easiest choice would be San Juan Beach Winery."

"That's a mouthful and kind of boring." She drummed her fingers on her knee. "I'll think of something clever."

"Did you think of Snap App?"

"I did. Catchy, isn't it?"

"It is." He turned the truck west toward the coast. "I'll take you to one of the newer places if you're up for seafood. There's a steak place, too, and they both do a breakfast or brunch or maybe even lunch."

"Seafood. I'm trying to rid my diet of red meat."

"Ethical or health?"

"I do love animals, but it's for health reasons."

He gave her a quick glance up and down. "You? You're as fit as you were in high school, when you were a soccer star."

"Soccer star?" she snorted. "Our team was awful."

"Yeah, but you were the best one on that awful team." He nudged her shoulder with the heel of his hand.

"You always were biased."

"I know. In my eyes, you could do no wrong—even when you did wrong."

Savannah tucked her hands beneath her thighs and sealed her lips. She'd done more wrong than Connor had known about, but why dredge up old skeletons? The new ones were keeping her busy enough.

She cleared her throat. "How much help do you have on the vineyard?"

"I have a chemist working for me, who drops by a few times a month. I have a couple guys who work the land daily, and I hired a marketing person who's going to help design the bottles, labels, logos—that kind of stuff."

Savannah wagged a finger in the air. "Don't let her choose the name of the winery. I have dibs on that—I mean, since we're back together and all."

"Don't take liberties."

"How long do you think we need to play kissy-face?" She dropped her gaze and pleated her skirt with restless fingers. A girl could hope.

"Kissy-face? You mean how long should we pretend to be a couple?"

She lifted her shoulders. "Same thing."

"We'll play it by ear. Let's see what the homicide detectives have to say. Let's see if you're their prime suspect." He gripped the steering wheel at the top with both hands, his knuckles blanching.

"Oh, God. Don't even go there. I don't want to think about it—any of it." She tipped her head, resting it against the window.

"Have you tried to remember what happened after you got to Niles's house?"

"I won't." She hadn't remembered the time before, either.

Connor's head jerked to the side. "Why so sure?"

"I—I don't know. That time last night just feels like a black hole. Besides, if I was roofied, I'm not going to remember. I don't think any victims after they'd been slipped Rohypnol ever remember what happened, do they? It's usually forensic evidence, rape kit, even CCTV and witnesses that help piece things together and lead to a conviction, not the victim's testimony."

"Typically, but why would Niles drug you?" Connor dragged a hand through his hair, tucking one side behind his ear. "He wasn't after you, was he? Wanting to get back together?"

"No way. He'd already moved on to a new girlfriend."

"Then why drug you?"

"I'm thinking it wasn't Niles who drugged me. Maybe somebody slipped something in both our drinks."

"At the bar?"

She nodded. "This the place?"

"How can you tell? The fishnets in the front or the giant swordfish?"

"Don't be a smart-ass." She punched his thigh with her fist and met rock-hard muscle. Being a vintner agreed with Connor—the longer, sun-bleached hair, the casual attire, his more relaxed attitude. The fact that he hadn't tossed her out on her bum after her outrageous story was a testament to that new attitude.

Although if she were honest with herself, she'd known Connor wouldn't turn her away. He never had even when she'd deserved it.

He swung the truck into a parking place around the side of the restaurant that fronted the ocean. "Tourists are out in force. That's the thing with these new restaurants. They do cater to the tourists."

"Is the food any good?"

"Would I take you out for bad seafood? It's decent."

"Maybe we should've gone to one of our old haunts with the old local crowd, like the Black Whale."

"Too risky. Too many direct questions. We need some time to ease into this."

When he turned off the engine, Savannah slid from the truck, yanking down her skirt as her sandals hit the asphalt.

Connor had come around to the passenger side. "Should've waited for me to help you out. The truck sits kinda high."

"I'm not going to hurt myself falling out of your truck." Connor might not be a cop anymore, but he hadn't lost his protective instincts. Thank God.

He took her hand. "It's showtime."

She was going to enjoy this role more than most of the ones she played. She squeezed his hand and bumped his shoulder with hers.

He opened the door for her, and she stepped into the restaurant, her breath hitching at the panoramic view of the ocean from the windows across the dining room. "Wow, no wonder this attracts the tourists."

"Hey there, Connor." A slinky hostess floated toward them, and Savannah moved in closer to her man, even if it was pretend.

"Hi, Cher. Do you have a table for two? No reservation."

"You don't need a reservation here, Connor. We have a no-show in the back, and that table has your name on it."

"Thanks, Cher."

As the resourceful Cher led them to the table with Connor's name on it, she twisted her head over her shoulder and winked at Savannah. "We're hoping to serve his first bottle of wine here someday soon."

"I can't wait for that myself. We're trying to come up with names for the winery right now."

Cher's eyes popped and a little stumble marred her sashay. She recovered nicely and pulled out a chair for Savannah. "Well, let us know when you decide. Enjoy your meal, you two."

Seated across from Savannah, Connor raised one eyebrow. "Laying it on a little thick, aren't you?"

She hunched across the table and grabbed both his hands. "We're back together. You're the man I ran to in the middle of the night, knowing you'd take me back."

The light from the window glimmered in his eyes as he studied every detail of her face. Could he see the truth there? She would always turn to Connor Wells in a crisis because he'd always be there for her.

He raised one of her hands, turned it over and pressed a kiss against the pulse throbbing in her wrist.

"Can I get you something to drink?" The waiter cleared his throat and asked again, "Drinks?"

Savannah tore her gaze away from Connor's and jerked her hand out of his grasp. The connection between them still sizzled, even under the current circumstances. It would never go away, but this was all still make-believe and she'd kept too many secrets from Connor to ever make this anything more than playacting.

"Since it's still before noon, how about a mimosa?" She ran a finger down a plastic drink menu. "The pomegranate mimosa, please."

"It's one of our most popular. And you, Connor? The usual?"

"That'll do."

Maybe nobody at this tourist trap knew Connor enough to ask probing questions, but they knew who he was. Everyone in San Juan Beach had known the Wells family. Her own mother had always told her to cozy up to Connor. The Wells family not only had position, they had money or at least land, which always translated into money.

She'd cozied up to him, but it hadn't been for power or money—and now she had plenty of the latter, thanks to Niles's death.

As the waiter walked away, Savannah tapped the side of her water glass. "The usual?"

"I've been doing a lot of wine tasting the past few years, and I found one I liked here." He shrugged. "I'm a creature of habit."

Savannah cranked her head over her shoulder at the loud voices coming from the bar. "Football game?"

Connor bolted upright in his chair, craning his neck toward the bar. "Not sure why they'd be pointing at us if it were."

As Savannah's gaze darted among the faces turned their way, she placed a hand against the fluttering in her belly. Was there news about Niles?

The bartender, Angel Cruz, burst through the low swinging door that led behind the bar and charged into the dining room. "Connor, there's a fire—at your place."

Connor jumped from the table, knocking over his glass of water. "The vines?"

"I don't think so, man." Angel tapped the cell phone in his hand. "My buddy said it's a structure."

"The house? Not the house." Savannah had tossed her napkin on the table and pushed back her chair.

"It's not the house, either. Some building on the property between the house and the vineyard."

"I'll settle this tab later." Connor swirled his finger above the table. "Fire department already there?"

"Yeah, yeah. Go, dude. Don't worry about this stuff."

Connor grabbed her arm and practically dragged her from the restaurant.

When they hit the parking lot, Savannah shook him off. "It sounds like it's under control, Connor, and thank God it's not the vines or the house."

"You don't understand, Savannah." He put his lips close to her ear. "The building that's burning? That's where I hid the knife."

Chapter Four

Connor raced back to his house, his truck flying over the asphalt. He'd be able to talk his way out of any speeding ticket right now.

Savannah sat beside him, twisting her fingers in her lap, worrying her bottom lip with her teeth.

She'd been mostly quiet after he told her about the knife in the burning building. She hadn't seen him put it out there, had she? Not that she had an opportunity to set a fire before they'd left for lunch.

He flexed his fingers on the steering wheel. "How the hell does a fire just start? There's nothing in that building like a heater or water heater or gas cans. It's just a storage area for now."

"A storage area that currently houses a murder weapon."

His hands jerked and the truck swerved. "What are you saying? There's no way anyone saw me hide that knife." Including Savannah.

He squinted at the white divider line on the road in front of him. "Besides, I thought your theory was that someone set you up for Niles's murder. How would that jibe with someone trying to destroy the murder weapon in a fire?"

"Destroy it? Is that what someone's trying to do? Maybe they're trying to expose us… me." She flicked her fingers at the window. "Firefighters swarming the place, putting out a fire, discovering a knife where a murder victim's ex-wife happens to be staying."

"I get you." He rubbed his aching jaw. "Why do you think I hightailed it out of that restaurant so fast? But intentional? How would this…arsonist even know you were here? How would he know I put the knife in the shed?"

Crossing her hands over her chest, Savannah said, "I don't know. What if the firefighters find it? Are they going to put two and two together when the news gets out?"

"Don't worry about it." He squeezed her bare knee, and then snatched his hand away.

How far would they take this pretense? He'd never been able to resist Savannah, despite his mother's warnings.

Like mother, like daughter. Mom always knew Dad had a soft spot for Georgie Martell, Savannah's mother, and when Dad wound up shooting and killing Georgie's husband to protect Georgie and Savannah, that had been the last straw for Mom.

As Connor turned onto the road leading to his property, Savannah tugged on his sleeve. "It looks like they're finished already…and there's a cop here."

"The sheriff's department always shows up with the fire department." He powered down the window and stuck out his arm.

The sheriff's deputy jogged to the truck. "You the owner?"

"Yeah, what happened?"

"Fire in that small wooden structure, not too much damage but you'll have to replace the roof."

"How'd the fire department get here so quickly?"

"You're lucky. Someone saw the smoke from the road and called it in."

"Cause?"

The deputy spread his hands. "Looks like arson."

Connor swore and Savannah stiffened beside him. "Now, who the hell would want to burn down my storage shed? Kids?"

"Maybe." The deputy swept his arm forward. "You can go ahead. They're wrapping it up, and the fire chief is going to want to speak with you."

"Got it, thanks." Connor pulled away from the deputy and rolled up his window against the smoky air. "Arson."

"This is freaking me out." Savannah

scooped up her purse from the floor and hugged it against her chest. "Why would someone set fire to the very shed where you just hid the knife that killed Niles?"

His gaze flicked to her face. "You're sure you weren't followed here?"

"I—I don't think so. Like I said, I ran home first to change clothes and throw some things in a bag. It was still early morning when I drove down here, almost dark. I think I would've noticed the headlights of another car dogging me on the road."

Connor rolled up the window and stepped on the gas pedal. "Don't be obvious."

"You mean we shouldn't run straight to… wherever you hid the knife and pull it out in view of the firefighters and deputy?" She rolled her eyes. "I think I can handle that."

He slid her a sideways glance. "I think you can handle a lot."

He pulled in front of the house, and an average-sized man who seemed overpowered by his gear tromped up to him, his heavy boots stirring up little clouds of dust with every step.

Connor mumbled under his breath, "The fire chief. Let me do the talking."

"It's your property." Savannah turned away and shoved open the passenger door.

Connor scrambled from the truck and thrust out his hand. "Chief, I'm Connor Wells and this is my property."

"Chief Murray." After shaking Connor's hand with his own gloved one, Murray jerked his thumb over his shoulder. "Arson. Crude Molotov cocktail. You know anyone who'd want to start a fire at your place?"

"Not a clue." Connor shoved one hand in the pocket of his shorts. "I'm just glad he decided to torch my storage shed instead of my vines."

Savannah had joined him and draped her arm casually around his waist. If she wanted to continue the pretense in front of the fire chief, who was he to complain?

"Yeah, that's unusual. Someone wanting to do you the most amount of harm would've started with your grapevines." Murray tipped his hat back from his forehead. "Maybe it was kids pulling a prank."

"In my day, pulling a prank would be playing ding-dong ditch, not setting fires."

Savannah pinched his side—hard. "That's probably what it was. They figured this was a worthless building with nothing much inside, so they wouldn't get in so much trouble if they were caught. I mean, as opposed to setting fire to the house or the land, which could've spread."

This time Connor nudged her sandaled foot with the toe of his shoe. If she kept going on and on about how worthless the shed was, she could raise the chief's antenna.

Connor cleared his throat, as much to stop Savannah from opening her mouth again as from the smoke lingering in the air. "I wouldn't say completely worthless. The shed isn't empty. Was anything inside damaged?"

"Singed a little, scorched…and now waterlogged, but the fire mostly damaged the roof, where the arsonist tossed the incendiary device." Murray stepped aside and waved his arm. "We've put it out completely, if you want to have a look inside, but don't go in yet. The wood's still hot and we're going to rip off that roof before we go."

Connor put his hand on Savannah's arm as she took a step forward. "Stay here. I'm just going to take a quick look."

He approached the blackened shed, water dripping from the roof, and one wall caved in. Ducking his head, he peered inside, his gaze wandering to the wine barrel where he'd stashed the knife.

A hand clapped on his back and Connor jumped and spun around.

Cole Miller, a friend of his, held up his hands. "Whoa, sorry, man."

"You're good. Just startled me."

"Yeah, who wouldn't be on edge? When I saw that we were riding out here to your property, I was hoping we wouldn't find the vines on fire. Glad it's just this storage shed."

"I had the same thought when Angel over

at Neptune's Cove told me there was a fire at my place—anything but the vines."

Cole hit the side of the shed with his hand. "Anything important in here? You have insurance, right?"

"Nothing much. I'm starting to collect some casks for the wine and some other stuff I'm going to need to construct my wine cave, and yeah, I do have insurance. I'm gonna need it to replace the roof and at least one side—unless my deductible is too high."

"Let me know if it is. My brother's still doing construction, and he'd be happy to give you a deal on the job." Cole squinted over Connor's shoulder. "Is that Savannah Martell over there looking hotter than the sun?"

"She's back."

"For you?"

"What else?"

"No telling with that girl." Cole blinked. "I mean, you know. Sorry, man. I'm glad if you two are back together."

"We are, and don't worry about it."

Cole coughed. "Did the deputy tell you we found some footprints around the perimeter of the shack? Flip-flops."

"Really? An arsonist wearing flip-flops?" Connor lifted his own foot. "Has to belong to the guy—or girl—who started the fire. I haven't been out here in flip-flops."

Another firefighter approached with an ax balanced on his shoulder. "We're going to start working on the roof now, Mr. Wells."

"Maybe I'll talk to the deputy to find out if the guy left any more clues." He nodded to Cole. "I'll catch you later."

Seeing his direction, Savannah, who'd been practically hopping from foot to foot, beat him to the deputy. When Connor reached them, she was asking about evidence.

The deputy answered, "We did find footprints around the shed—flip-flops."

"One of the firefighters told me that. They're not mine."

"Not mine, either." Savannah pointed to her sandals. "Does that further point to teenagers?"

The deputy shrugged. "San Juan is a beach town. A lot of people wear flip-flops—some all year long."

"But to set a fire? It's looking more and more like kids to me."

Connor interrupted to shut her up. "Did you find anything else?"

"The jar used for the Molotov cocktail was one of those ones that people use to preserve fruit. My grandma used to do that, and I recognized it from a piece of glass."

The sound of a blade splitting wood cracked through the air and Savannah grabbed his arm.

"They're taking the roof down. Do you need me for anything else, Officer? I'm going to make some calls to my insurance company and maybe my friend's brother to find out if he can do the repairs."

Savannah dug her fingers into his biceps. "We're not going to stay out here and watch them demolish the roof?"

"You can keep an eye on them if you want,

Savannah. I'm going to make those calls, if there's nothing else."

"One more thing." The deputy adjusted his equipment belt. "How come you never applied to the sheriff's department after the San Juan PD went away? I'd heard you were a good cop."

"That was six years ago. I'm surprised you remembered." The familiar knots tightened in Connor's gut.

"I never forgot that story about how those drug dealers went after your father, the chief, when he killed Manny Edmonds. That was some crazy stuff for this small town."

Connor's jaw tightened. "That situation didn't have to end with my father's murder. He'd been warning the sheriff's department about Manny for years, and nobody listened to him."

The deputy took a step back and a bead of sweat formed on his brow. "Didn't know that."

"It's ancient history." Connor rolled his shoulders and patted the phone in his pocket.

"I'm going to make those calls now. Are you going to watch the demolition, Savannah?"

She nodded, her lips pressed into a thin line.

Connor pulled his phone from his pocket and strode toward his house.

Savannah didn't like being reminded of that ancient history, either, as Manny had been her mother's husband, and Connor's father had killed Manny to protect the Martell women.

His father had admitted to him later, and only because Connor had overheard a conversation between him and Georgie, that the kill hadn't been in self-defense. He'd killed Manny in a fit of pure rage over what he'd been doing to Dad's town…and what he'd been doing to Georgie Martell, which seemed the stronger motive. And Georgie and Savannah had lied to protect him, claiming Manny came at him with a weapon. They'd even planted Manny's gun in his hand.

Connor slammed the front door behind him and perched on the edge of a stool at the granite island. If he were honest with himself, his father's admission had done as much to sour him on police work as his death had. It had destroyed Connor's trust in authority in general and his father in particular.

He wiped a trickle of sweat from his face and placed the first call to his insurance company.

About forty minutes later, Connor stepped onto his front porch, and Savannah, standing several feet from the shed and talking to Cole, waved her arms over her head to signal him.

Cole always did have a thing for Savannah.

Connor stepped off the porch and joined them. "All done?"

"Yeah, Chief Murray was just going to get you. Any luck with the insurance company?"

"They're going to send out an adjuster tomorrow."

One of the firefighters called out from the rear of a fire engine, and Cole waved back.

"Looks like we're all done." Cole touched Savannah's shoulder. "Welcome back, Savannah, and my condolences on your ex-husband's…death."

"Thank you, Cole." She patted his hand, still resting on her shoulder.

Cole tromped back to his truck, his gear making him look a lot bigger than he really was.

Connor took a step forward to stand beside Savannah, his shoulder bumping hers. "You told him?"

"Wouldn't I? I talked to Dee today and she told me. He'd think it odd once he found out about Niles…and he will find out. Everyone will."

"You're right. Quick thinking." In fact, all Savannah's instincts so far had been right on—as if she'd rehearsed them. He rubbed two fingers against his temple. "Everything go okay out here otherwise?"

As she waved at the departing sheriff's deputy, a tight smile on her face, she said, "They knocked down the roof, tore out the damaged wall, but didn't touch anything inside."

"They didn't divulge any more clues to you as to who set this fire?"

"Nope. All they have is the piece of jar from the Molotov cocktail and the flip-flop prints. Doesn't exactly narrow it down."

"But doesn't point to anyone following you here and trying to draw attention to the hidden knife. It didn't work anyway."

"Speaking of the hidden knife." She tapped his shoulder. "Shouldn't we check on it?"

The dust from the last emergency vehicle to drive through the gate settled, and Connor hacked out a breath that seemed to have been trapped in his lungs ever since they drove onto the property.

"Let's look." He turned and walked toward the damaged shed, with Savannah hot on his heels. As he ducked inside, his nostrils twitched at the smell of the soggy, burnt wood.

Savannah followed him in and stood in the middle of the space, hands on her hips. "At least with that entire wall down, we don't need a flashlight, and it's not unbearably hot. It must get dark in here at night."

Connor grabbed a large screwdriver from a pile of tools on the floor, covered with ash, and pointed it at the wine cask at the end of a row. "I put it in there."

He took two steps toward the hiding place and jimmied the spigot off the front of the cask. A flutter of fear whispered across the back of his neck before he thrust his hand inside.

"Well?" Savannah whispered the word in his ear, even though they were the only ones in the shed.

His fingers grasped the knife's handle, crinkling the plastic bag around it. "Still here."

"Thank God." She grabbed a handful of his T-shirt. "Let's get it out of here before the insurance adjuster and the construction workers descend tomorrow, or before the arsonist decides to come back and toss another homemade bomb at it."

Connor eased the bag out of the cask. "I think I can find another place for it."

"We can't just destroy it? Get rid of it?" Savannah clamped down on her bottom lip with her teeth.

"It has blood on it, evidence. It might have the blood of the killer on it. You'd want to know that, wouldn't you?" A muscle ticked at the corner of his mouth.

"Of course, unless…"

He cinched his fingers around her deceptively fragile wrist. Savannah had always been one of the strongest women he'd known. "You said you couldn't have done it, even though you blacked out. No blood on you, no evidence, only those superficial wounds on your hand."

"That's *not* what I was going to say." She twisted her arm out of his grasp. "Maybe my blood *will* be on that knife because the killer used it to cut my hands."

"Either way, I don't want to destroy this evidence if it is the murder weapon. We don't even know if it is." He cocked his head. "Did you hear that?"

"No. I can't hear a thing over that giant fan the fire department left to dry the water."

Connor cupped her elbow and steered her out of the shed. As they stepped outside, a dark Crown Vic rolled up and a man in a suit jumped out of the passenger side of the vehicle before it even came to a complete stop.

Savannah murmured out the side of her mouth, "Who the hell is this?"

A cold dread dripped down Connor's spine, as he clutched the plastic bag with the knife in front of him.

The man in the suit adjusted his dark sunglasses and brushed some dust from the lapel of his jacket. "Savannah Wedgewood?"

"Yes, Savannah Martell, actually." Her body had stiffened beside Connor's and her fingers pinched the material of his shirt at the side.

"I'm Detective Krieger from the San Diego Sheriff's Department, Homicide. This is

Detective Paulson. We're here to ask you some questions about the murder of your ex-husband, Niles Wedgewood."

Chapter Five

The detective's words acted like a sledge-hammer to her solar plexus. She'd been expecting this visit, had been almost anxious to get it over with. But not while Connor was standing next to her with a bloody knife in his hands, bag or no bag.

She swallowed and opened her mouth, but her tongue and throat were too dry to form words.

Krieger's bushy eyebrows jumped to his hairline. "I'm sorry. You knew about your husband's death, didn't you?"

"I—I did. His assistant, Dee Dee Rodriguez, told me earlier today." She placed a hand against her stomach. "Just hearing it again punched me in the gut."

"I'm sorry."

She slid her arm around Connor's waist, her fingers touching one edge of the plastic bag in his hands. "This is Connor Wells."

"Mr. Wells."

Krieger stuck out his hand, and Connor released the bag and took it.

"We just had a minor catastrophe on my property—a fire."

The other detective stepped around the sedan, planting his black wingtips in the dirt. "Yeah, we saw the fire engines on our way in. Much damage?"

"Just a storage shed, nothing important and no injuries." He waved the bag toward the house. "Would you like to come inside to conduct this interview?"

"Thanks." Krieger gestured for his partner to follow Connor first, twisting his head around to survey the scorched shed.

Savannah swallowed hard and tried to

avert her gaze from the plastic bag swinging from Connor's fingertips.

Krieger's gaze slid to Savannah's face. "Quite a day."

"Oh, that." She flicked her fingers toward the shed. "Nothing compared to Niles's death."

Krieger bowed his head, and she moved in close behind him as if to block the shed from his view and his mind. The way Connor was waving that bag around had her heart skipping beats. He couldn't excuse himself to hide it, but he'd better watch it or that knife would come flying out of the bag and land at the detectives' feet—and then they'd be in real trouble.

She stumbled on the first step and bumped into Detective Krieger's suited back. "Sorry."

"Are you okay?"

"Rattled. Like you said, this *has* been quite a day."

The detectives' hard-soled shoes clattered on the wood floor as they maneuvered around the living room to take their seats.

"Something to drink?" Connor pulled out the trash drawer and placed the bag with the knife inside.

Krieger declined and Paulson requested a water.

Savannah didn't dare look at the detectives and check if they'd noticed Connor throwing away the bag. Why wouldn't he pick up some damaged items from the shed and dispose of them in the trash?

She smoothed her sticky palms against her skirt as she sat on the edge of the couch. The detectives had claimed the two chairs facing the couch—like an inquisition. They just needed the bright light.

Connor returned to the room with a glass of water for Detective Paulson and one for her. "Here, babe. Your throat's probably scratchy from the air outside."

Connor was jumping right in with their little deception. He used to call her babe when they were together. She tapped her fingers at the base of her throat. "You're right. It is."

She took a sip of water and then folded her

hands around the glass, balancing it on her knee. "What can you tell me about my ex-husband's murder, Detective Krieger? Dee Dee, Niles's assistant, didn't have much information and I read only a small blurb online."

"He was stabbed to death, Mrs… Ms…?"

"You can call me Savannah, but I did return to my maiden name, Martell." The cuts on her palm tingled. "Stabbed. How horrible."

"I gather you were the last person to see him. You two had a drink last night at the Marina Sports Bar?"

"We did, yes."

"Purpose of the meeting?" Krieger's gaze shifted to Connor and back.

"Business."

"You still own Snap App together. Is that right?"

"We do." She wasn't going to point out the obvious fact that the company belonged to her now—lock, stock and barrel.

"Your meeting was about Snap App?"

"It was."

"Cordial?"

The corner of her lip twitched. "Not really, but no different from any other discussion Niles and I had—married, separated or divorced."

"What was the reason for the divorce?" Again, that subtle shift of attention from her to Connor.

"Infidelity—his."

Paulson cleared his throat. "What happened when you left Niles, Savannah? Where did you go? What did you do? When did you last see Niles?"

So, Paulson was the one to get to the nitty-gritty. Would he be the one to slap on the cuffs?

"We left the bar together. I got into Niles's car with him to finish our discussion, he drove me to the corner and then I walked home. That's the last time I saw him." The ice in her glass tinkled as her hands trembled.

Paulson's gaze dropped to her glass. "You walked home from the bar?"

"I walked *to* the bar, also. It's less than a mile to my house, and I wanted to clear my head. That's when I decided to come down here to see Connor—and that's what I did."

"You didn't see your ex or hear from him after that?" Paulson hunched forward, so far that Savannah could see the freckle on his earlobe.

"I didn't, but there's something I don't understand." She tucked a strand of hair behind her ear. "Was Niles murdered in his home?"

"In his bedroom."

She placed the glass on the coffee table and pinned her hands between her knees. "We had security cameras at that house. I know because I hired the company and oversaw their work. Wouldn't Niles's murderer be caught on tape?"

Krieger shook his head. "The security cameras were disabled."

"Oh." Savannah covered her mouth with her hand.

"We're not even sure the killer is responsible for disabling the security system, because Ms. Rodriguez thought Niles was having problems with the system. Did you ever have problems with that system?"

"Not when I lived there."

Paulson drained his water and tapped the glass with one finger. "Mr. Wells, what time did Savannah arrive at your house last night?"

Savannah's heart pounded so hard the buttons on her blouse trembled. Surely, Paulson and Krieger could hear it beating.

"She came in around eleven o'clock."

Paulson asked, "Were you surprised to see her, and at that time of night?"

"No." Connor reached over and stroked Savannah's wrist with the pad of his thumb. "We'd been talking about getting back together. Her meeting with her ex last night was the final straw, I think. The thing that finally convinced her we belong together."

She grabbed Connor's hand and kissed the back of it. How would she ever repay him for this?

Paulson scratched his chin. "So, you two

were together from about eleven o'clock last night until now?"

"Except for the few hours I went to the beach this morning," Connor said.

Paulson scooted forward in his seat. "What time?"

"Around eight to ten. Left Savannah sleeping. Wait." Connor ran a hand through his longish hair and the ends flipped up. "You're not looking at Savannah for this, are you?"

"What? Are you?" Savannah knotted her fingers together. "Wh-why?"

Krieger raised his shoulders to his ears. "Exes, acrimonious divorce and business deals. It's natural we'd look at you."

"Not natural to me." Savannah jumped up from the couch, grabbing her water, which sloshed over the side of the glass.

Connor pushed to his feet and placed his hand at the small of her back. "You'd better show the detectives your hand, Savannah."

Her head whipped around and her eyes widened. Was he trying to get her arrested? "M-my hand?"

Krieger and Paulson exchanged a look that made her stomach flip-flop.

Paulson stood up first, and Savannah tilted her head back to look at him. Funny, she hadn't noticed how tall he was when he was the silent partner. Now that he was grilling her, he towered over her like an ogre.

Connor grabbed her right hand and un-curled her fingers, displaying the horizontal cuts on her palm.

Krieger's eyebrows, which seemed like they had a mind of the own, cocked in two different directions. "What happened, Savannah?"

"Oh, this?" She stared at her hand. "I was straightening up a bit before I left last night and my butcher block of knives tipped off the edge of the counter. I stupidly made a grab for the knives and cut myself. Pretty dumb move, huh?"

"It's quite common for someone to get cuts on their own hand while they're stabbing someone." Paulson crossed his arms.

"Only one problem with that, Detective." Connor planted a kiss in the middle of her palm amid the cuts. "Savannah is left-handed. She wouldn't have stabbed her ex, but she really wouldn't have stabbed him with her right hand."

Paulson's chest seemed to deflate. "We're going to want you to come to the sheriff's station in La Jolla in the next few days to give a sample of your DNA. Can you do that?"

"Of course."

Krieger put one hand in his pocket as if to strike a casual pose. "Would we find your DNA in the house, Savannah?"

"DNA? Blood? No. Hair? Maybe." She flipped her hair over one shoulder. "I've been in that house a few times recently...for business. I don't think it would be odd to find some evidence of my presence, but blood? There would be no reason for my blood to be there."

She hoped to God they wouldn't find any from these cuts.

The detectives asked her several more questions, handed out their cards and asked her not to leave town and to report to the station in La Jolla the day after tomorrow in the afternoon.

She assured them she would, and both she and Connor walked them to the front door.

Her muscles still clenched, she watched them descend the porch, and just when she thought she could breathe again, Paulson made a half turn.

Tapping his chin, Paulson raised his eyes to the sky. "Wells. You *are* the son of the former police chief of this town who shot and killed the drug dealer Manny Edmonds, aren't you?"

"That's right. Shot and killed him in self-defense and then paid the price when Manny's goons murdered him."

"Hmm." Paulson took a few more steps, stopped and twisted his head over his shoulder. "And Manny Edmonds was your step-father, wasn't he, Savannah?"

"That's right."

"You were present when Chief Wells killed him."

"I was."

"Hmm. Okay. Thank you."

Paulson stopped again, his hard shoes scraping against the gravel as he pivoted. "One more thing."

"Of course." Savannah could barely squeeze the words past her lips.

"Do I have your permission to search the trunk of your car?" Paulson linked his hands in front of him as if he'd just asked her for a cup of tea.

She stretched her lips into a smile. "Of course. I'll get the keys."

Her shoulder banged against Connor's as she spun toward the house, but she avoided meeting his eyes. Why did they want to look in her trunk? Thank God Connor had found that bag...and too bad he'd been waving it around under the detectives' noses.

She dragged her keys from her purse with shaky fingers and took a deep breath. She couldn't allow Paulson or Krieger to see her trembling hands.

As she stepped out onto the porch, she stabbed the remote with her thumb and the lights of the Lexus flickered once and the trunk popped. "It's open. Help yourself."

Paulson lunged toward the car and flipped up the trunk. Half his body disappeared inside, and Savannah knew he was lifting the cover to the spare—where Connor had found the bag.

She forced herself to breathe—in, out, in, out—Connor's body vibrating beside her.

Paulson extricated himself from the trunk, glanced at Krieger and gave a quick shake of his head. "Okay to look inside the car?"

"Absolutely. It's unlocked."

Paulson rummaged around her car for several minutes, and then emerged, the tight politeness of his face somewhat askew. "Thank you. That's all."

Detective Krieger nodded and waved.

"Thank you for your time. Sorry for your loss."

"No problem. Let me know if I can be of any more help." Savannah gritted her teeth as she watched the two detectives walk back to their vehicle.

Connor touched her shoulder. "Let's go back in the house. We look weird standing here staring at them, making sure they get back in their car and drive off."

"But that's exactly why I *am* staring at them, just in case Paulson stops and asks another one of his casual questions dripping with suspicion and innuendo, or decides he wants to see what's in that plastic bag you were swinging around." She peeled her hands from her upper arms, where her fingernails had created crescents in her flesh.

Connor held the screen door open for her and she stepped into the house, massaging the back of her neck. "Why do you think he wanted to search the car? The trunk? How did he know?"

"Maybe he didn't know about the knife." Connor's shoulders twitched.

"You don't believe that any more than I do. Someone tipped them off. The same someone who put the knife there."

"Might've been an anonymous call."

Savannah rubbed her eyes. "How do you think it went otherwise? Do you think I'm their number one suspect?"

"Maybe not number one, thanks to your alibi, but definitely a suspect."

She dropped onto the couch cushion and leaned her head back, staring at the ceiling. "Why do you think Paulson threw in those little jabs at the end? Is he implying that there's a connection to my being at the site of one killing and Niles's death?"

"Why would he imply that?" Connor peered into her face from above. Placing two fingers at each of her temples, he rubbed in little circles. "The death of your stepfather has nothing to do with the death of your ex-husband."

She hoped it didn't.

Closing her eyes, she said, "The two of us involved in two separate violent deaths—must look odd."

"He's just trying to rattle you."

Connor stopped his massage, and she opened one eye. "Why would he want to do that?"

"Because you're a suspect and he wants you to know you're a suspect, and he wants you to understand that he's looking at you, has already looked into your background."

"And finds it suspicious." She tapped the side of her head. "Keep rubbing. I suddenly have a ferocious headache."

"Probably because you haven't eaten anything all day. Do you want to go back to Neptune's Cove and continue our lunch date?"

"We do want the locals to think we're back together and inseparable, don't we?"

"That's the plan."

That plan sounded like heaven right now. Too bad it was all tied up with Niles's murder.

Connor's fingers trailed down her face and

the column of her neck before squeezing her shoulders. "Okay, let's try this again."

Did he mean lunch or their relationship? Because being back in Connor's realm felt good, felt natural. But she'd left him because of the lies and the lies hadn't gone away. In fact, they'd been compounded by more lies. She didn't want to start a relationship based in deception, even though that had been the only way her mother ever started a relationship.

She wasn't her mother and never would be. She also couldn't afford to tell Connor the truth.

She ducked away from Connor's touch and staggered to her feet. "I'm starving and I could use that mimosa now more than ever."

As she reached for her purse, her cell phone, tucked in the side pocket, rang. She pulled it out and glanced at the display. She met Connor's urgent stare and held up the phone. "It's just Letty, Niles's housekeeper."

She answered the phone. "Letty, are you all right? I heard about Niles today."

"Did you?"

Savannah drew her brows together. "Dee Dee called me and I just talked to the police. Have they spoken to you yet? Do you know anyone who would do this to Niles?"

"As a matter of fact, I do. It was you, Savannah, and I have the evidence to prove it."

Chapter Six

Savannah jerked her head up, her eyes widening in her pale face. Connor's stomach dipped. What bad news could Niles's housekeeper be telling her? He mouthed, *"What's wrong?"*

She tapped her phone's display and a woman's slightly accented voice came over the line. "Well? What do you have to say?"

"I—I don't know what you're talking about, Letty. I had nothing to do with Niles's murder. Why would you even think that?"

Connor's hands convulsively clenched into fists. Why would Niles's housekeeper think Savannah killed him?

"Oh, you forget, Savannah. I was in that

house for the fights. The cheating. The lying," Letty snorted. "I don't even blame you. I felt like killing Mr. Niles myself a few times. He didn't treat me any better after you left."

"Letty, don't even say something like that." Savannah shot him a glance and licked her lips. "And during any of those…fights, did either of us get physical? Did I ever threaten Niles? Of course not. Yeah, I wanted the man out of my life, but the divorce was good enough."

"The divorce was not good enough. You still had the company together and would always have to work with him or let him buy you out. I know how these things work. I overheard the two of you enough times."

Connor folded his arms over his chest, biting the inside of his cheek. He didn't need a recap of Savannah's marriage—he'd tried not to think of it over the years. Savannah needed to know what Letty had on her…and what she wanted now.

"Whatever." Savannah flung her arm out

to the side. "None of that means anything now. I did not kill Niles and I can't imagine what proof you have that I did."

"I'm not going to tell you that, Savannah, not yet, but I'll give it back to you when we meet…and you hand over five hundred thousand dollars."

Savannah's gaze met Connor's and her lips tightened. "That's what this is all about? I never took you for that kind of person, Letty."

"We all have to do what we have to do."

"Yes, but I didn't kill Niles, so you don't have any evidence."

"You'll see. Come alone, bring the money, in cash, and I won't contact the police about what I found and what I know."

"Letty, this is ridiculous. If you need money, I'll give you money. You don't have to resort to blackmail, which is illegal, I might add."

"So call the police."

Savannah ran a hand through her hair and clenched a fistful of it. "Where and when do you want to meet?"

"Logan, by the warehouses. There's one with a yellow sign out front. Be there at nine o'clock tonight with the cash. I'll turn over your property and we'll call it even."

"I'm only doing this because I don't want the police looking at me. I didn't kill Niles, Letty, and you must know that."

"I know what I know."

Savannah opened her mouth to respond, but Letty had ended the call, and Savannah threw the phone at the couch and screamed.

"What does she have, Savannah?"

"I have no idea. I didn't leave anything there." She paced to the window and spun around. "I can't believe she's doing this. Blackmail."

"Does she have some grudge against you?"

"We weren't besties or anything, but it was Niles she didn't like."

"Why?"

Savannah pleated her skirt with her fingers. "Because he's an ass and rude."

"Why'd she continue to work for him?"

"He paid really well, or at least I paid Letty

well, and Niles had to keep the agreement with her when I left."

"Greed. She's doing this because she can. Because she knows you'll pay."

"If it's something ridiculous, I'm not going to pay her a dime." She clapped a hand over her mouth. "How am I going to pay her five hundred grand in cash? I have about forty bucks and change on me and if I run to the bank now and withdraw that kind of money, it's going to raise all kinds of red flags with the police."

"I'll take care of the money. I'd just like to know what she has first."

"I told you, if it's something that can be explained away easily, I'm not paying her anything, and she can go to the police for all I care. She's going to have a helluva time explaining to them why she didn't turn over this explosive evidence when they first questioned her and decided to turn to blackmail instead."

Connor shook his head.

"What?" She narrowed her eyes. "You don't think I should pay her? If it's the money you're worried about, I'm good for it. Haven't you heard? I'm the beneficiary of millions in life insurance money."

He inhaled deeply through his nose. When had Savannah become so difficult? He rubbed the back of his neck. Who was he kidding? After her stepfather died, she'd changed, and he could never figure out why. It wasn't as if she blamed Connor's father for Manny's death. She'd never cared for Manny, but when he died, something between them…shifted, and they'd never been able to set it right again.

Why would this time be any different?

"I don't care about the money. Haven't you heard? I inherited a lot of property when Dad died and I sold off a lot of it to finance the winery." He briefly clutched his hair into a ponytail and then released it. "I'm just beginning to think you're getting in deeper and deeper. Maybe you should just tell the truth."

For once.

Her mouth dropped open. "You're kidding. You know as well as I do the truth isn't enough sometimes—and this is one of those times. Someone incapacitated me and probably Niles, too, and then murdered Niles, leaving me to hold the bag. This is some kind of setup. If I go to the police, you can bet there will be more evidence popping up to implicate me."

"Could it be Letty?"

"You think Letty could've murdered Niles and then tried to set me up for this blackmail scheme?"

He shrugged his shoulders, which ached with tension. "Could be. She's the first one who stepped forward to cash in."

"I know she hated Niles, but murder?" She strode to the couch and swept up her phone. "I don't think she's capable."

"She thinks you are."

Savannah pointed her phone at him. "She

doesn't, really. She just found this clue—whatever it is—and figured I'd pay to make it go away."

"And that's exactly what you're going to do."

BY THE TIME Connor found a new hiding place for the knife, cleaned up and withdrew the cash from his bank before closing time, their lunch date had turned into dinner.

He stuffed the backpack loaded with stacks of money under the table at his feet and smiled at a different waiter from the one they'd had earlier in the same restaurant. "I'll have the Widow's Peak pinot."

"And I'll have the pomegranate mimosa... again." Savannah planted her elbows on the table.

Connor raised an eyebrow. "It's not breakfast anymore."

"Are there mimosa rules that I missed somewhere?"

He tipped his water glass in her direction.

"You make up your own rules, Savannah. You always have."

"I like the hair." She tugged on her own glossy ends. "Now that you're no longer a cop, you decided to grow it long?"

"Honestly, it's pure laziness. Do you remember Lucy, who used to cut my hair? She left town, and every time someone new cut it, they just couldn't get it right."

"Lazy." She rolled her eyes. "You don't have a lazy bone in your buff bod."

"Tell me how the company's doing. I mean—" he waved his napkin before flicking it into his lap "—outside all the other stuff."

"The other stuff? You mean the murder of the CEO?"

"Yeah, that."

She cocked her head and caught a drip of condensation on the outside of her water glass with the tip of her finger. "Not as well as it should be."

"Really?" He coughed into his napkin.

"That's not what I've been hearing...and that's not how the stock is going."

"You're following Snap App's stock?"

"I'd better be. I own a lot of shares."

"Oh, then I'd better work harder."

"Seriously, what's the problem?"

"Earnings seem to be going down."

"Again, that's not what the stock price is reflecting."

"I know."

The waiter returned with their drinks and paused by the table. "Everything okay out at the vineyard, Connor? We heard about the fire."

"Thanks, Brock. It was just a storage shed. Firefighters put out the fire pretty fast, so there wasn't much damage."

"I heard it was done on purpose." Brock glanced over his shoulder. "Any suspects?"

"Not yet." Connor swirled the wine in the glass. "Any ideas?"

"Yeah, I have an idea."

Connor's fingers curled around the stem of the glass. "Are you serious?"

"Dude, I heard you were filming the Cove Boys this morning."

"Who?" Savannah had been listening to their exchange, her head turning from side to side, as if she were watching a tennis match.

"Some localism going on at the cove. You know, pushing out other surfers from different areas." Connor turned back to Brock. "That's right. I was filming them this morning. You hear something?"

"Just that Takata was pissed off and talking trash."

"Enough to start a fire?"

"Maybe." Brock rapped his knuckles on the table. "Gotta get back to work. I'll come back around."

"Thanks, man." Connor tapped his wineglass against the rim of Savannah's champagne flute. "Cheers."

"To what, exactly?" She sipped her bubbly drink and scrunched up her nose.

"We may have discovered our arsonist."

"Jimmy Takata's become some rabid surfer?"

"You know how localism goes. These guys think they own the best waves on the beach and drive everyone out. People started calling them the Cove Boys, and several are suing them."

"And you decided to get involved in it?" She traced the rim of her glass with her fingertip. "Why? You're not a cop anymore."

"The sheriff's department won't do anything about it."

"Not your problem, Connor. Can't help yourself?"

"I hate to see that kind of stuff going on in this town." He took a longer pull from his glass than he intended under Savannah's amused eyes.

"So what happened this morning?"

"I was at the cove, helping out the lawsuit with my camcorder, and Takata didn't like it."

"He threatened you?"

"I don't know if I'd call it a threat, but he got aggressive."

Savannah snapped her fingers. "That could

be it, couldn't it? We were so worried that someone followed me here and set fire to the structure to smoke out that…object, and it could just be a local problem."

"We don't know for sure if it's Takata."

"Sounds promising." She stared at him over the rim of her glass. "Why didn't you think of that before, when the deputy asked you if you had any enemies?"

"I don't think of Jimmy Takata as my enemy. If it was him, that's a pathetic attempt at intimidation."

"Maybe, but it is criminal. That can't help his case any."

"I'll call tomorrow and drop his name." He held up his glass to the candlelight. "If I could make something like this at my vineyard, I'd consider that a success."

"Widow's Peak?" She placed a hand against her chest. "Maybe it's some kind of sign. I guess I'm a widow."

"Technically, not. Niles was your ex."

"I wish I hadn't encouraged him to keep that life insurance coverage. It looks bad."

"It all looks bad, Savannah, but in the end, if you didn't do it, you'll be okay."

"You don't believe that."

He took another sip of wine, savoring the blackberry taste on his tongue before swallowing. "Tell me more about the company. You know I couldn't be prouder of you for what you've built."

A rose tinge that matched her drink touched her cheeks. "Thanks, Connor, but it wasn't all me. Niles had a brilliant mind and was able to realize all my imaginings."

"I know." He pinged the side of his glass with his fingernail. "I always thought if I'd had something like that to offer you, I could've made you stay."

Her hand shot out and she grabbed his wrist. "It wasn't like that at all. Things just got...complicated between us. I know your mom hated me—and I totally understood it. My mom had no right to embroil your father in her problems."

Connor's mouth twisted up at one corner. "I don't think my father could've kept away from Georgie if he'd tried, and besides, he was the chief of police. He had a duty to help her."

"You and I both know Chief Wells wouldn't have gone to those lengths for anyone other than my mom."

Savannah still had hold of his wrist, and he slipped it out of her grasp and threaded his fingers through hers. "I'm just sorry it had to affect us and what we had."

"I heard you two were back together."

Connor jerked his head to the side and nodded to Savannah's best friend in town, Lexi Morris.

Lexi dipped down and gave Savannah a one-armed hug. "So glad to see you back here. I heard about Niles. I'm so sorry. So horrible and scary. Are you worried someone could be coming after you, too?"

"I don't think his murder is related to the company, but I do feel safer down here with Connor." Savannah brought his hand to her lips and kissed his knuckles.

"And you." Lexi prodded his shoulder. "I heard there was a fire at your vineyard."

"Just a small one. Nothing much damaged."

"Typical for you two." Lexi rolled her eyes. "Drama dogs you everywhere. I'll be following the news of the murder. I hope they catch the killer. Niles wasn't my favorite person in the world, but nobody deserves that."

"I hope so, too. Are you having dinner with Zach?" Savannah craned her neck, twisting her head to take in the dining room.

"We're finished." Lexi made a face. "I'll tell you about it later. Just meeting a few friends for drinks at the bar, but let's catch up soon. Lunch?"

"I'll call you." Savannah kissed the tips of her fingers and waved them at Lexi as her friend turned back to the bar.

"She didn't seem surprised to see you here, or see us together." Connor took a deep breath. Maybe this was going to be easier than he thought.

"No, she didn't. Didn't even ask when I

got here." She pushed her water glass to the side. "Food's here."

Connor dug into his fish and chips, and after Savannah squeezed lemon over her grilled salmon, she snatched one of his fries and popped it into her mouth. "Mmm."

He pointed his fork at her. "I don't know why you just don't order your own fries."

"It's more fun stealing yours, and if they're not mine the calories don't count." She grabbed another one to prove her point.

While they ate, he asked her more questions about the business. She'd majored in computer science at San Diego State and had met Niles there. He hadn't been worried about Niles at the time because Savannah had assured him she and the computer geek, as she'd called him, were just friends.

But after his own relationship with Savannah had unraveled, Savannah and Niles began spending more time together and she'd come up with this idea for a social media app. They'd put it to work, formed Snap App, made millions and got married, or got married and made millions.

And there had been nothing he could do to stop any of it.

Now Niles was dead and Savannah stood to gain control of the entire company—and that life insurance money.

"Enough about me." Savannah dabbed her mouth with her napkin. "How's the winery coming along? It looks like you have fruit on those vines."

"I need to wait one more year before harvesting the grapes and making wine. The plants need to go through a few growth cycles before they're ready to produce wine."

"You mentioned you have a chemist. Have you decided on the formula or recipe or whatever you call it?"

"Yeah, Jacob is finalizing it now." He tapped his chin. "You missed a spot of tartar sauce."

"Can't take me anywhere." She swiped at her face with the napkin, missing it again.

Connor hunched forward and swept his

fingertip across the spot of white sauce. He brought up his thumb and pinched her chin. "You're as beautiful as ever, Savannah. You sweep in here and spellbind me, wrap me up in a web until I don't know if I'm right side up or upside down."

She fluttered her long lashes, not even denying the compliment like most women would. "D-does that mean you regret helping me?"

He dropped his hand and dropped his voice, pushing away his empty plate. "No. I do owe you. If you and your mother hadn't lied to the police and told them Manny drew his gun on my father first, Dad would've been arrested for murder, or at least manslaughter."

She coughed and gulped down the rest of her water. She glanced at the diners nearest to them, absorbed in their own conversations. "If you hadn't agreed to give me an alibi for Niles's murder, it's not like I would've reported your father. It's water under the bridge now."

"But you still brought it up when you asked for my help."

Savannah dropped her chin to her chest and looked at him from beneath her long lashes. "I regret that. I never meant to call in the favor. I knew you wouldn't turn me down."

Connor clenched a fist against his thigh beneath the table. He couldn't figure out which was worse—Savannah using an old favor to bring him to heel or her understanding that she didn't have to use anything at all to make him come around.

"I'm coming with you tonight when you meet Letty, even though she told you to come alone."

"You'd better stay out of sight. I want to see whatever she's got so I can gauge how worried I need to be."

"You don't need a worry gauge." He drilled his finger into the table in front of her. "The fact that someone thinks she can blackmail you should cause you enough concern— whatever she has."

"It does, believe me. That's why I'm meeting her. How much time do we have?"

Connor rolled his wrist inward. "About an hour, but it'll take us almost thirty minutes to drive up there. I'm not familiar with Logan. What kind of area is it?"

"Sketchy—some residential, some light industrial with a whole lot of abandoned warehouses, and that's where we're meeting."

"Great. Why do you think she picked that spot?"

"It's isolated, no witnesses, and I believe she lives out that way."

"So, Letty might have reinforcements on her side."

"She's not going to hurt me, Connor. She just wants the money."

"Everything you thought you knew about Letty went right out the window when she decided to use this information against you. She could be plotting anything."

"I think she's planning to nab the cash and quit working as a housekeeper. I almost admire her." Savannah buried her chin in her hand.

"What?" Connor bolted upright in his chair. "She's a criminal about to commit an illegal act, already committed that act by calling you."

"True, but that was some quick thinking on her part to jump on a piece of evidence and turn it to her advantage."

"Save your admiration until you find out what she has. Seems like an immoral money grab to me."

"Of course. I'm not condoning her actions, especially because they're aimed at me. I'm just marveling at the realization that you never really know anyone, do you?"

Uneasiness churned his gut. And what about Savannah? Did he really know her? She'd changed from the girl who'd been raised by an economically struggling single mother. The girl who'd mastered everything she did to prove she was as worthy as all the kids who lived in comfort and ease in their idyllic beach community.

Her current wealth had given her a different kind of confidence. The founding of Snap App had afforded her more wealth, several times over, than any of the kids she used to try to impress.

"Well, I'm ready to find out what she has." Savannah threw her napkin on the table beside her plate.

"Let's get the check." He waved at Brock, who was heading for the bar to pick up a drink order.

On his way past their table, a tray of drinks balanced on one hand, Brock slipped their bill onto the table and tapped it with one finger. "See you next time."

Connor put his knuckle on the check. "I'll get this," he said to Savannah. "You don't want to start spending money like you have it."

"I do have it—even without full ownership of the company and Niles's life insurance."

"I know." He pinched the bill between two fingers and squinted at it in the low light. "I'm just kidding."

She nudged his toe beneath the table. "That's nothing to kid about. Once those detectives find out all I stand to gain from Niles's death, they're going to come calling again."

"They may know by the time you go in to give your DNA sample, and they probably put in a request for your phone records already." He pulled some bills from his wallet and placed them on the tray.

"I liked it better when you were kidding." Savannah hitched her purse strap over her shoulder. "Do you think they'll find it odd that my phone was off during the crucial time?"

"Maybe. There's not much they can do about it, though." He grabbed the bag with the money and hitched it over his shoulder as he stood up from the table. "Ready?"

"As much as I'll ever be."

They said goodbye to a few people on the way out, and Connor kept his explanations of the fire brief.

When they got inside the car, Savannah

turned to him. "How are we going to do this? If Letty sees me with someone, it might scare her off."

"You can drop me off at a distance and drive my car in. Just pick me up on your way out. If there's trouble…get to the car and honk the horn."

"Yeah, that's the problem with skulduggery. When you're leaving your cell phone at home, there's no way to get in touch."

As he started the engine he slid a glance her way. Had she expected skulduggery the night Niles was murdered? Was that why she'd left her phone at home?

"Just be careful."

"I know Letty."

"We went through this before. You *thought* you knew Letty. This is a different person you're dealing with now."

"You're right." She twisted around and smacked the money bag with her hand. "Do you want this bag back?"

"Of course. I'm not leaving any evidence with Letty that we paid her off. Any self-respecting blackmailer is going to bring her own bag for the money."

"And if she doesn't?" She tugged her skirt over her thighs. "Then what?"

"That's her problem. She can dump the cash in the back seat of her car. Don't let her leave with the bag."

"Got it."

They discussed a few more logistics on the way to Logan, and when he exited the freeway, Savannah pointed to her right. "Take this street down to the T in the road and then hang a left. You might want to park there and turn over the car to me."

"Remember, park as close to the warehouse as you can. This doesn't look like the kind of area where you want to be loitering."

"You, either." She tapped on the window. "You can wait at that gas station. There's even a convenience store."

"Great. I'll get some coffee and thumb through the smutty magazines."

She squeezed his thigh. "You don't read smutty magazines."

"Who said anything about reading?"

"I give you points for trying to lighten the mood, Wells."

"Just be careful." He swung into a parking space at the side of the service station and turned the wheel over to her.

He watched the taillights until they disappeared as Savannah turned right onto a side street. He strode around the corner of the building and entered the convenience store, where he bought a cup of coffee.

Then he pushed out of the front door and took off in the same direction as Savannah and the car. He had no intention of waiting out this meeting in the store. He'd try to keep out of Letty's sight, but he didn't really give a damn about what she wanted. The woman was blackmailing someone who'd employed her, paid her well and, if he knew Savannah, had treated her well, too.

He picked up the pace as he turned down the side street and spotted the warehouses crouching at the end of the cul-de-sac. As he drew closer, he couldn't see a yellow sign and he couldn't see any cars.

He wove through the first row of buildings and tripped to a stop when he saw two cars parked in front of a hulking warehouse with a corrugated metal roof.

He watched from the corner of another building, but seeing no movement, he crept forward with his heart thumping in his chest. How long could this exchange between the two women take?

As he drew closer to the building with the yellow signage, he cocked his head, listening for voices. The silence caused a ripple of fear across his flesh.

He placed his hand on the metal door, which was standing open several inches, and hunched forward, peering into the cavernous space of the warehouse. The moon filtered through some broken windows, creating a muted spotlight around two figures—one crouching and the other sprawled out on the floor, a dark pool beneath her head.

Chapter Seven

Savannah flinched as her hand brushed Letty's clammy skin while she searched her front pocket.

A soft creak echoed in the warehouse, and Savannah spun around on her knees, placing one hand on the cold cement floor as she listed to the side.

"Savannah! Are you all right? What happened?"

She released a breath and staggered to her feet. "Connor, what are you doing here? Not that I'm not glad to see you. It's Letty. Sh-she's dead."

Connor strode across the floor, stopping

short of the dead body between them. "What happened here?"

"I don't know." She wrapped her arms around her midsection. "When I got here, I saw Letty's car out front and then I came inside and saw her body on the floor. It's a gunshot wound. She has a gun in her hand."

Connor crouched next to Letty, his gaze darting from the gun in her hand to the gaping wound at her temple. "She killed herself?"

"That's what it looks like."

"Or that's what someone wants it to look like." He jabbed a finger in the air over the body. "What were you doing when I walked in here?"

Savannah swallowed. "I—I was looking for the evidence she had. I know it sounds sick, but that's what I came here to get."

Connor's jaw tightened and her stomach sank. She plucked at the material of her skirt. "I realize it sounds awful, but I spent several minutes in shock just staring at Letty, and several more minutes trying not to be sick."

"And then several minutes searching her pockets."

She closed her eyes and drew a deep breath. "That's what we came here for, Connor. We were willing to hand her five hundred grand for whatever she has. Just because she… killed herself, I'm not going to leave without it."

"You don't really believe she killed herself, do you? She was just about to score an easy five hundred thou."

"But if she didn't—" Savannah flattened a hand against her belly, afraid this time she really would hurl "—who did kill her and why?"

"To stop the blackmail plan."

"Who'd want to do that…except me?" She swept her arm to encompass the warehouse. "And I just got here."

"Did you find what you were looking for?"

"I found nothing." She poked at an empty duffel bag with the tip of her sandal. "Except this. You were right. She was ready to collect the money."

"Did you look in her car?"

"No. Should we?"

"We're not going to do a search, but let's take a look before we get out of here."

Savannah hoisted the bag with Connor's cash, and he took it from her.

"You didn't leave anything in here?"

"No. I walked in with the bag, saw Letty, rushed over and dropped the bag. I was very careful with what I touched and how I touched it, and I didn't lay a finger on the gun in her hand."

"Okay, you're getting to be an expert at this."

Savannah convulsively clenched her hands at her sides. Connor had no idea how right he was.

He pushed the warehouse door wide with his toe and slipped into the night. She followed.

With his T-shirt over his hand, Connor opened Letty's unlocked car door and did a quick scan of the front and back seats. "I don't see anything. Either she was lying... or someone took it."

The blood rushed to Savannah's head and she swayed, grabbing Connor's belt loop to steady herself. "What do you mean?"

"Let's get out of here." He tipped his head back and studied the outside of the building. "I'm guessing these warehouses are too old and too dilapidated to have any kind of security or camera system."

"I can't imagine why they would, and I doubt Letty would've picked this place if she thought our meeting could be caught on CCTV."

"You drive." He gave her a little nudge toward his car. "Let's go."

She slid into the driver's seat and squeezed the steering wheel with her hands to keep them from shaking. She drove out the way she'd come in, neither of them saying one word until she hit the freeway.

Then she turned on him. "Why would

someone kill Letty and then take the evidence she had against me?"

"To have the evidence against you."

She licked her dry lips. "Do you think I'm going to get another blackmail demand?"

"I don't know."

"Or worse? Someone wanted Letty's evidence to continue my setup."

"We don't even know what Letty had and if it was damning enough to send the detectives your way." He smacked the dashboard. "Who knew about this meeting? Do you think she told someone? Does she have a family?"

"She has a husband and some adult children. I doubt her husband knows anything about the blackmail scheme." Savannah shifted her gaze to the rearview mirror. "Do you think someone could be following me?"

"How? You said yourself nobody followed you down here. I know for a fact nobody tailed us to the warehouse. Maybe someone is following Letty. Whoever killed her got to the warehouse before you did. How long do you think Letty had been dead?"

"I have no idea. I didn't touch her, and I wouldn't have known what to look for if I had."

"Did you smell gunpowder in the warehouse? I detected a faint whiff, but it can hang in the air for a while."

"I didn't notice any gunpowder smell—don't even know what it smells like. The warehouse smelled oily to me anyway. It could've been gunpowder."

"You weren't late." Connor drummed his fingers on his knee. "How did someone beat you there and kill Letty before you got there?"

"You're still assuming someone killed Letty." She lifted her stiff shoulders. "Maybe it was a suicide. How do we know what's going through anyone's mind? Maybe she even killed Niles and was regretting everything."

"A few hours ago, you assured me Letty couldn't have killed Niles."

"What do I know?" She pinched the bridge of her nose.

"Not much of anything. You don't even know what happened that night."

She cranked her head slowly to the right and stared at his profile. "Are we back to that? I know I didn't kill Niles. I would've had blood on my clothes, and if you're going to suggest I murdered him while I was naked, I checked the bathroom for signs of a shower. Hell, I even sniffed my own armpits for evidence I'd cleaned up—and I hadn't."

"Look." He placed a hand on her thigh. "Don't you think you should see a therapist to get to the bottom of it?"

His hand felt heavy through the thin material of her skirt, and she tensed her leg muscles. "I didn't black out from any suppressed memory from a traumatic event. I was drugged. There's no coming back from that. No memories are going to return from a drugged state."

"You sound so sure. You have no proof of any drugs. You would've had to have been drugged in the bar, and that's unlikely. I think we agree Niles didn't drug you."

She tapped her fingers on the top of the steering wheel. "Maybe he did."

"You also told me before he had no reason to knock you out, as he wasn't interested in getting you into bed."

"He could've had a different motive."

"A killer is either waiting for Niles or breaks into his house, finds you conked out, murders Niles and proceeds to strip you of your clothes and put you to bed?"

"To set me up." She flung her hand at the windshield. "Just like this thing with Letty."

Connor shook his head. "We need to take a step back from the speculation and focus on Letty's death back there. Assuming she didn't kill herself, how did her killer know about her meeting?"

"My head hurts." Savannah massaged her right temple. "She must've told someone."

"Maybe she's working with someone and that person double-crossed her."

"This is going to look weird, isn't it? The

fact that Letty's employer is murdered and then she's murdered? What are the chances?"

Connor held up his index finger. "But Letty's death was made to look like a suicide. The gun's in her hand, a single gunshot to the head. Unless the killer left some evidence or Letty has some defensive wounds, this might go down as a suicide. The detectives might think she had something to do with Niles's death."

Savannah closed her eyes briefly and then focused on the white lines skimming by outside the windshield. She hoped Letty's death was ruled a suicide, to give them a little breathing room. She needed room to breathe.

Later, as Savannah turned down the road leading to Connor's house, she asked, "Those detectives are going to want to talk to me about Letty, too, aren't they, whether or not they deem it a suicide?"

"I'm sure they will."

"If they're going to be looking at her phone records, I'd better tell the cops that Letty called me today to discuss Niles's murder."

"Be as truthful as you can."

Whipping her head around, she said, "I'm not telling them I was there that night, Connor. It's too late for that anyway. I could be charged for...for leaving the scene of a crime, not reporting a murder or whatever they can dig up. That's not happening."

"I said as truthful as you *can* be."

As she brought the car to a slow roll in his driveway, Connor unsnapped his seat belt. "Park to the right of the truck."

Several minutes later, when they were in the house with the door locked behind them, Connor grabbed his phone from the counter, studied the display and held it up to his ear to listen to a message.

Savannah paced, twisting her fingers, and when he put the phone down, asked, "What was that about?"

"Don't worry. Just the fire chief letting me know they were reporting the fire as arson for the purposes of my insurance claim."

Savannah dropped to the couch and aimed the remote at the TV. She regretted it immediately when Niles's handsome face and slick smile filled the screen. "Story's exploded."

Connor walked up behind her and placed a hand on her shoulder. "We knew it would. No surprises."

"Yeah, the surprise is going to be when someone discovers Letty's body."

"I wonder when that's going to happen." He squeezed her shoulder briefly before releasing it. "Those warehouses look like they haven't been used in years."

"Her family will report her missing." Savannah pressed her fingers against her lips. "Why did she get involved in blackmail? She'd be alive right now, home with her husband, if she hadn't got greedy."

"Did you notice if she had a phone on her?"

"She didn't. Was there one in the car?"

"Not on a charger or anywhere else I could see."

She muted the TV as the news shifted to another story. "Maybe she's playing the same game we are—leave your phone home so the police can't trace it."

"Her family's not going to be able to trace her, either, if she didn't have her phone with her. Unless she told someone where she was going, which is unlikely, her body might be there until someone looking at the warehouses sees her car and discovers her."

Savannah dug her fingers into her scalp. "That's horrible. I can't bear to think about it."

"And yet—" Connor folded his tall frame into the chair across from her "—you were willing to leave Niles at his house, dead."

"That's different." She slipped out of her sandals and wedged her bare feet against the coffee table. "Niles was at his home. I knew someone would be discovering him, and that someone happened to be Letty—bad luck for her as it turns out."

"She sealed her own fate by taking something she thought incriminated you and then trying to sell it back to you."

Savannah rubbed her upper arms, where a trail of goose bumps had sprung up. "So you do believe that's why Letty was murdered and now someone else has that evidence."

"Maybe." He hunched forward, driving his elbows into his knees. "We just have to wait for the other shoe to drop."

"That's encouraging, thanks."

"Or…"

Her head popped up. "Or?"

"We do a little investigating of our own. I still have some connections and a little know-how. You're familiar with the players and have more money than you know what to do with. Let's launch our own investigation, independent of the police."

"If it can help me out of this mess, I'm all for it."

"We'll start a list of…suspects tomorrow morning."

"Suspects? I don't know anyone who'd want to kill Niles."

"C'mon, Savannah. The guy must've had enemies. He cheated on you with other women. Do you think he changed his behavior?"

"I'm sure he hadn't." She drew up her knees and wrapped her arms around her legs. "Niles was the kind of guy who was geeky throughout high school and college, and then became attractive all of a sudden when he made millions."

"That's understandable, but the dude was married—to you." Pushing out of the chair, Connor snorted, "Crazy bastard."

Savannah's cheeks warmed and a smile tugged at one corner of her mouth. She was glad Connor still felt that way, even though she'd done a number on his head.

He pivoted and leveled a finger at her. "I have one condition."

"Shoot."

"You make an appointment with a therapist and see if you can remember anything about that night."

Savannah swallowed a lump in her throat. "Really?"

"I mean it, Savannah. You lost several hours of your life, and you owe it to yourself to get those back."

"I'd have to admit to the therapist that I was there, in that room with Niles's dead body."

"They're bound by confidentiality, and I can refer you to someone, someone you can trust." Connor folded his arms. "That's the condition."

"All right, but I don't think it's going to do any good. Those memories are gone for good." Just like those other memories buried in her past.

"Okay, then. Investigation starts tomorrow." He swept her cell phone from the counter and held it out to her. "I think it's safe to turn this on now."

She rose from the couch and took the phone from him. "I'm sure it needs to be charged again. I wasn't lying when I said the thing dies all the time."

He jerked his thumb over his shoulder. "The sheets are clean in the guest room. Remember to make the bed every day so nobody gets suspicious that you're sleeping here as a guest. I'm going to see if there are pillows in there."

She watched through narrowed eyes as he headed for the back rooms. Maybe she hadn't expected him to sweep her off her feet and carry her to his room…but she sure wanted it.

Sighing, she hopped up to sit on the stool at the counter and attached her phone to the charger. It buzzed in her hand, and she glanced at a stream of text messages filling up her screen.

A glimpse at the first message told her the news of Niles's death had spread like a cancer. She dutifully tapped each text, reading the messages of shock and condolence, her tongue wedged in the corner of her mouth. Even Mom had sent her a text—a cryptic one, of course.

One of the last messages, one from an unknown number, had a picture attached to it. Savannah tapped it and swept her fingers over the picture to enlarge it.

Her gut twisted and she dropped the phone.

"Savannah, what's wrong?"

She turned toward Connor, gripping the edge of the counter as her world tilted. "Someone sent me a picture of a button."

"A button?" Connor's brows snapped over his nose.

"It's the evidence—Letty's evidence against me."

Chapter Eight

Connor ate up the space between him and Savannah in two long strides and caught her by the shoulders as she listed to the side. He smoothed a hand down her rigid spine.

"Let me see." He reached over her and scooped up the phone, the picture of a colorful button still enlarged on the display. "This is your button? Do you even know if it's missing?"

Nodding, she cleared her throat. "When I got dressed at Niles's, I noticed the button on my blouse was gone. It's pretty distinctive, so I got down on my hands and knees to search for it and found it beneath the dresser.

I—I thought I dropped it in the pocket of my slacks."

"You haven't seen it since?"

"I forgot about it. I stuffed my slacks in the laundry basket in my closet when I got home after I left Niles's place." She bowed her head, tugging at the roots of her hair.

"If you never looked for the button, it could still be in your pocket."

Her head shot up, and then the light died from her violet eyes, turning them into dark pools. "You think Letty or someone else planted that button in Niles's bedroom? It's too unique. I bought that blouse in Paris. There's no way somebody found a duplicate for that button."

"Okay, okay. It's the same one." He wedged his hands against the counter, dropping his head between his arms.

The fact that Savannah had been careless enough to let the button fall out of her pocket gave him a glimmer of hope. She'd been so cold-bloodedly precise about everything else—her phone, her car's license plates, her fingerprints. This detail finally pointed to a woman frantic and caught off guard by the murder of her ex-husband.

"There's no text accompanying the picture? No demands?" He brought the phone close to his face and backtracked to the message with no words. "The number says Unknown. I suppose Letty's killer wouldn't be dumb enough to call you from his...or her real phone."

"If he's not blackmailing me, what does he want?"

"What he *didn't* want is for you to have that button back." Connor placed the phone on the counter and rubbed his chin. "But how did he know about that meeting? How did he know Letty had the button?"

"Maybe he's working with her and decided to keep all the ransom money for himself."

"Husband?"

"No way."

He cocked an eyebrow in her direction. "Spouses have murdered each other for a lot less than five hundred grand."

"I don't know. Maybe you're right." She pushed off the stool and stumbled. "It has to be someone she told, because only you and I knew about the meeting with Letty. Nobody followed us. Nobody followed me down here."

"You're sure about that?" He shoved his hands in his pockets, resisting the urge to reach out and steady her. If he touched her, he'd take her in his arms and never let her go—and that wasn't his best course of action right now, no matter how much he wanted her.

"I'm sure. There wasn't much traffic at that time of the morning, and believe me, I was watching for anyone trailing me."

"I do believe you." He tapped the phone. "Get rid of that message and let's call it a wrap. Your bag is in my room, so I'll give you some time to get ready for bed. It's been one helluva day."

Savannah dug her fists into her eyes and rubbed, smearing mascara and eyeliner across her cheeks. "Are you sorry I showed up on your doorstep? Where Savannah Martell goes, trouble follows. That's what you used to say."

"I did?" He huffed out a breath. "I guess nothing's changed, but I'm not sorry you showed up. Where else would you go?"

An hour later, Connor lay on his back in his large bed and stared at the ceiling. Would he be able to help Savannah out of this mess? Did he want to?

He had to face the possibility that she'd killed Niles in self-defense and had blocked it out. It had to have been self-defense.

He squeezed his eyes shut and rolled over.

A FOOTFALL WHISPERED behind her, and Savannah dropped half an eggshell into the mixture in the bowl.

"Jumpy, aren't you?" Connor reached over her shoulder and plucked out the shell with two fingers. He tossed it into the sink, dripping egg white on the kitchen tiles.

"Don't make a mess in here." She whisked some pepper into the eggs and milk. "You didn't have any bacon or sausage in the fridge. Scrambled eggs and toast okay?"

"Fine, but you didn't have to cook breakfast." Connor ripped a piece of paper towel from the roll and swiped at the spot on the floor.

"I owe you…big-time. A little breakfast barely makes a dent in that debt."

"There's no debt owed here, Savannah." He leaned against the sink, his hands gripping the counter behind him.

Her gaze skimmed over his body, drinking in every inch of him, his board shorts hanging low on a pair of slim hips, his tight abs dusty gold from the sun. She'd fallen for Connor Wells the first time she'd laid eyes on him back in middle school. After Mom's second divorce, she'd moved the two of them from the mountains of Colorado to the sandy beaches of California.

Once Savannah got a glimpse of Connor, all her resentment toward her mother over the move vanished.

Connor had taken to her as well, teaching her how to surf, easing her transition to a new school, a new lifestyle. Life had been good—until Mom met Manny.

Connor snapped his fingers and she blinked. "Earth to Savannah. Where did you go?"

"A little trip down memory lane." She turned back to her eggs and whipped them into shape.

"Ahh, the good old days." He squeezed past her and grabbed a tub of butter from the fridge. "You wanna hop on a board while you're here?"

"Let's see." She placed a fingertip on her chin and rolled her eyes to the ceiling. "I'm under investigation for the murder of my ex, just missed the murder of my former housekeeper and I'm living under the threat of blackmail. Who *wouldn't* want to go surfing? I thought I was the irresponsible one here."

He shrugged and scooped a couple pats of butter from the container and dropped them into the frying pan. "Those things will still be true whether you're riding the waves or not."

"I thought we were going to start investigating today."

"We are, as soon as you call Thomas Bell."

"Thomas Bell?"

"The therapist."

She clenched her jaw as she prodded at the butter now sizzling in the hot pan. Connor was like a dog with a bone.

"That's the deal." He nudged her in the back.

"All right. Leave me his number." She dumped the egg mixture into the pan. "Friend of yours?"

"He is…now."

"Now?" She stirred the eggs in the skillet and then blinked at the congealed yellow mess. "He was *your* therapist?"

"That's right." Connor crossed his arms, widening his stance.

"Oh, I didn't know…" As her cheeks heated up, she shifted the pan from the fire to another burner. But she could've guessed. Connor had lost a lot in a short span of time—his father, his job, his mother…and her.

Although his life was an open book to the people he held near and dear, he wasn't the kind of guy to bare his soul to just anyone. He must've been in bad shape to turn to a professional.

"It wasn't my idea. After Dad was murdered and the sheriff's department started taking over the San Juan PD, they sent me to Thomas as a condition of my employment with them."

"But you didn't work for the SDSD." Connor had quit police work in disgust after Manny's cohorts had killed Chief Wells.

"I was considering it, so I saw Thomas for a few sessions and then I continued with him." He turned away from her and reached into the cupboard for a couple plates. "I never thought seeing a therapist would have any value for me. I was wrong. Thomas is a good guy and he knows what he's doing."

"And yet—" she slipped two pieces of

bread into the toaster "—you never went back to law enforcement."

"Thomas helped me with that, too. I came to terms with my decision and realized my life had to take a different direction."

"Now, that *does* sound like therapy talk." She waved the spatula at him.

"Guilty." He held up the two plates. "Eat at the counter okay, or do you want to sit at the kitchen table?"

"Let's sit at the table. It's such a pretty view." She couldn't wiggle out of this therapy thing, but she didn't have to tell Thomas anything. The therapist would have to maintain her confidentiality with his good friend and former patient, Connor, too.

As she buttered the toast, Connor reached around her and scooped half the eggs onto one plate and half onto the other.

"There's marmalade in the fridge for the toast."

"And salsa for the eggs?"

"You know me. Can't eat eggs without salsa."

She *did* know Connor. He'd always been open, friendly, up-front. She'd been shocked by his open manner when she'd first met him. She figured everyone had family secrets, things you just didn't tell anyone—her mom had drilled that into her enough times. But then her mother had so much to hide in her own past.

And now Savannah did, too.

She spun around from the refrigerator, clutching a jar of salsa in one hand and a jar of orange marmalade in the other. "We're good to go."

As they sat across from each other over toast, eggs, juice and coffee, Connor had to spoil the moment.

"Have you looked at your phone yet this morning?"

"Of course."

"Anything more from the blackmailer?" He heaped some salsa over his eggs and offered her the spoon.

"If only we knew for sure he *was* a black-mailer. I haven't heard anything from him...

or her. What does he want? Why would he go to those lengths—murdering Letty—to get that button? I could've dropped that button at any time in Niles's house."

"But you didn't. You were wearing that blouse the last night Niles was alive, so you would've had to have lost it the same night—and you told the police you didn't go to the house." Connor tapped her plate with his fork. "If they catch you in one lie, they're gonna look at you even more closely."

She dragged the tines of her fork through the runny salsa on her plate. "What do you think those detectives are doing right now?"

"They might be requesting your phone records. They might be checking the Marina Sports Bar, verifying your story."

The toast she'd just eaten rumbled in her stomach. "Most of that checks out."

"If there's CCTV outside the bar, how's that going to look?" Connor snapped a piece of toast in half.

"It will show me and Niles leaving the bar together and getting into his car, if the camera is pointing that way. I told the detectives we got in Niles's car, so that's not a problem." She shredded the paper towel next to her plate. "The problem is that button, or at least the person who has the button."

"I don't see how he—"

"Or she."

"—or she can use that button to blackmail you now. He'd have to sneak back into a crime scene and plant it."

"That's what Letty would've had to have done, although at least she'd have a reason to be at the house."

"In Letty's case, she could've told the police she found the button at the house, picked it up without thinking and then realized later it was yours and it had significance."

"I suppose so." Savannah dropped her fork, along with the pretense of eating, and dragged a pad of paper toward her. "You wanted me to start a list of people connected to Niles, and I think the first one on that list has to be Tiffany James, his girlfriend."

"First—" Connor fished his phone from

the front pocket of his shorts "—you're going to call Thomas and make that appointment."

She held out her hand. "All right, although I don't think it's going to do any good."

"Humor me." He smacked the phone against her palm.

Connor had left Thomas Bell's contact info on the display and she tapped the screen to place the call she'd been dreading. She eased out a breath when it went to voice mail.

"Hi, Thomas. My name is Savannah Martell. I'm a friend of Connor Wells, and I'd like to make an appointment to see you."

Connor poked her arm and circled his finger in the air.

She stuck her tongue out at him. "As soon as possible. You can call me back on Connor's phone. Mine is acting up. Thanks."

She ended the call and shoved the cell back across the table toward Connor. "Happy?"

"Very." He aimed his fork at her plate. "Are you going to finish those eggs?"

"I don't have any appetite at all. How you

can eat after what we saw last night is beyond me."

"Really?" He dumped more salsa onto her plate. "Last night when you were going through Letty's pockets, you didn't seem that squeamish."

"I was doing my best not to vomit." She'd had the same gut-wrenching feeling when she saw Niles's wounds, but Connor seemed to think she was some coldhearted schemer—and he didn't even know the half of it.

"It's a good thing you didn't." He corralled the rest of her eggs with the last corner of his toast. "I don't have much sympathy for blackmailers anyway."

Before they finished cleaning up the kitchen, Thomas Bell called Connor back.

"Thanks for returning Savannah's call so quickly, Thomas. I'll give the phone over to her."

Savannah dried her hands on a kitchen towel and took the phone from Connor. "Hello."

"Savannah, this is Thomas Bell. I can get

you in as early as tomorrow, if that works out for you. I just had a cancellation."

"Sure." She licked her lips. "What time?"

"Eleven o'clock."

"I can do eleven." She could do any time. What did she have going on except the fight of her life to prove her innocence?

Thomas gave her the address of his office, even though she knew damned well Connor would take her and probably escort her inside.

She put down the phone. "There. That's done. Now I think we need to go see Tiffany today."

"Won't she think that's strange?"

"I have a reason to see her, one she won't mind."

An hour later, they were on the freeway up to San Diego, and Connor asked, "How come Tiffany didn't live with Niles?"

"Honestly, I think it's because Niles found it easier to cheat on her if they kept their separate residences."

Connor shook his head. "The one time I met Niles, he did not strike me as a player."

"That's because you met him before Snap App's stock went public and the money really started rolling in. All that money sort of made him like a pro athlete—without all the muscles. Once women found out who he was and what he was worth, they threw themselves at him." She shrugged. "He had a hard time resisting."

"Did Tiffany throw herself at him?"

"In the most blatant way possible. Tiffany's a stripper... I mean, an exotic dancer."

Connor's mouth dropped open. "Niles was going to marry an exotic dancer?"

"I don't think Niles had any intention of marrying Tiffany, despite the big ring he gave her."

Connor whistled. "Niles was playing with fire. Once the detectives discover all of this, they're going to have a few more suspects to look at than you."

"Then I'd better make sure they know about Niles's cheatin' ways."

"Especially if Tiffany doesn't tell them herself." He tapped her phone, which was charging on the console. "Aren't you going to call her?"

"I didn't want to give her a chance to say no." She swept her finger across the display on the dash to make a phone call. "But now we're almost there. How can she refuse?"

The ringing of Tiffany's phone filled the car and just when Savannah got ready to leave a message, Tiffany answered, her voice breathless.

"Savannah? Is that you?"

"It is. How are you doing? I'm so sorry about Niles."

Tiffany's voice broke on a sob. "It's horrible. I can't even get out of bed."

"How did you find out?"

"The police came to my front door and told me." Tiffany sniffled. "I can't believe it. D-did the police talk to you? They want my blood or something."

"They did question me and they want my DNA, too. It's not a big deal, Tiffany. I'm sure they're going to ask everyone close to Niles…just to rule us out."

"I'm shocked and just heartbroken." Tiffany paused to blow her nose. "Do you think I can keep the ring?"

Connor rolled his eyes at Savannah, but she wasn't about to judge Tiffany.

"Of course. Niles gave it to you." She maneuvered the car onto the next off-ramp—the one that would take her to Tiffany's condo. "In fact, I need to talk to you about a few things, Tiffany. Can I come over right now?"

"Right now?"

"I'm in the neighborhood, right around the corner, actually."

"Oh. Okay."

The car's speakers amplified some whispering and rustling noises on the other end of the line, and Savannah raised her brows at Connor.

"You can meet me at the pool. It's toward the back of the complex."

"See you in about fifteen minutes."

Savannah ended the call and drummed

her thumbs on the steering wheel. "Did that sound to you like she didn't want us in her place?"

"That's exactly what it sounded like. I thought she couldn't get out of bed."

Savannah lifted her shoulders. "Maybe the place is a mess."

Fifteen minutes later, Savannah pulled her car into the parking lot of the sprawling condo complex.

"Exotic dancing must pay well." Connor shaded his eyes as he peered out the window.

"I'm sure you can guess Niles bought the place for her."

Savannah parked where she could find a spot marked for visitors. When she got out of the car, she tugged on the wrinkled legs of her shorts. "At least we're dressed for the pool."

They followed a path through lush landscaping and Savannah inhaled the scent of jasmine as the sun warmed the back of her head. This could all be so pleasant, especially with Connor by her side, if she weren't trying to figure out who was framing her for murder.

They turned a corner and faced a fenced pool area scattered with chaise longues, the blue water lapping at the sides of the pool. Connor breathed out. "Nice."

"Wish we were here to enjoy it." Savannah tried the gate, but it didn't budge. She hung on to the bars and pressed her face between them, spotting Tiffany stretched out in the sun. "Tiffany!"

Niles's girlfriend turned her head, her bleached blond hair piled on top, and waved.

Before she could stir herself, another woman pushed out the gate and held it open. "Friends of Tiffany?"

"We are, thanks." Connor caught it and ushered Savannah through. "You first."

Savannah's flat sandals slapped the cement as she approached Tiffany, whose eyes were hidden behind a pair of huge sunglasses.

"Thanks for seeing me, Tiffany. You'll be glad you did."

She started to nod and then her head

snapped back when Connor came up beside Savannah. She scooted her dark glasses down the length of her nose. "Hello there."

"Tiffany, this is Connor Wells. Connor, Tiffany James."

Tiffany held out a limp hand, her long fingernails glittering in the sun. "Hi, Connor. Nice to meet you."

He squeezed her fingers in an awkward handshake. "Same here. If you ladies don't mind, I'll stake out this chaise longue over here and soak up a few rays."

"So, you're the famous Connor Wells." Tiffany shoved her glasses back up her nose, and a little smile played about her full lips.

"Famous?" Connor grabbed the hem of his T-shirt and yanked it over his head, putting his rippling torso on full display.

Savannah couldn't see Tiffany's eyes behind her sunglasses, but she didn't have to see them to know where the woman had focused her gaze.

"Oh, Niles may have mentioned you a few hundred times."

"Sorry for your loss." Connor stretched out on the chaise longue as if he didn't have a care in the world.

Savannah knew he'd be listening to every word the two of them said.

Tiffany's mouth immediately curved down. "Thank you. It was a shock."

Savannah pulled up the chair between the two recliners now inhabited by Tiffany on one side and Connor on the other. "Do you have any idea who would want to kill Niles?"

"Besides you and me?"

Savannah sucked in a breath. "That's not funny, Tiffany. I hope you're not telling the detectives that."

She waved her long nails in the air. "No, but he was a cheatin' dog, wasn't he? The cops are gonna learn that, even if we don't tell them."

"I had ceased to care about Niles's cheating."

"Did you ever care?" Tiffany shoved her sunglasses to the top of her head and shifted her gaze to Connor, lounging behind her.

Savannah scooted to the right to block her view. "Did Niles tell you anything about problems he was having, or any enemies?"

"No." Tiffany narrowed her eyes. "Is that what you came here to ask me? Are you workin' for the popo now?"

"Just curious." Savannah bent forward and straightened a strap on her sandal, dipping her hand into Tiffany's bag at the same time. "I really came to see you to make sure you contact Niles's attorney, Chris Neelon. Niles definitely left you something in his will."

"He did?" Tiffany's lips parted. "How much?"

"That, I don't know. That's why you have to call Neelon. I wanted to make sure you knew about Niles's will."

"Do those detectives have to know that?" Tiffany flicked her fingers in the air at a young man in a white shirt and slacks crossing the pool deck.

"It's a murder investigation. They'll know everything like that."

The man stopped in front of Tiffany's

chaise longue and flashed a set of white teeth in his brown face. "Pool-side massage, Ms. James?"

"Yes, Diego. Can you set that up and I'll be over in a few minutes?" She glanced at Savannah. "If we're done."

"We're done. Just wanted to let you know about Niles's will and see if you had any ideas who killed him." Savannah twisted around in her chair. "Are you ready over there, sun worshipper?"

Connor opened one eye and rubbed a hand across his chest. "Feels good."

"I can have Diego set up another massage, if you like." Tiffany sat forward and tugged her swimsuit cover-up from her impressive body.

Connor didn't even blink. "We'd better get going. We wouldn't want to disturb you in your mourning."

Tiffany's nostrils flared. "What's done is done."

Savannah pushed up from the chair and

raised her hand. "I suppose I'll see you at the funeral—whenever they release the body."

As Tiffany stretched out again like a cat, they sauntered across the pool deck and swung open the gate.

When it clanged behind them, Connor took Savannah's arm. "That didn't tell us much."

"Maybe Tiffany didn't tell us much, but her condo will." Savannah held up the key chain she'd swiped from Tiffany's bag. "But we'll have to make it fast before she notices it's missing."

"You're kidding." Connor dropped his shirt on the ground.

"While some of us were flexing our muscles in the sun, some of us were working."

"We'd better hurry up in case she changes her mind about succumbing to Diego's magical hands." As Connor bent over to sweep up his shirt, he turned his head toward the pool. "Do you know her condo number?"

"I've seen it enough on Niles's papers and correspondence. It's 246."

Cupping Tiffany's key chain in her hand,

Savannah strode down the path that led back to the units, with Connor right beside her—as it should be. She'd missed having him on her side. He gave her confidence and an unshakable belief that everything would turn out for the best—even when she strongly doubted that, like now.

They walked upstairs to Tiffany's corner unit, and as Savannah slid the key into the lock, Connor stood behind her, keeping watch.

She pushed open the door and stepped inside, the smoky air making her blink. She whispered, "I thought she gave up smoking. That was a deal breaker for Niles."

"Niles isn't around anymore, is he?" Connor nudged her inside and clicked the door behind them.

Savannah put her hands on her hips and surveyed the messy room. "Why wouldn't she want us in here?"

"Are you expecting to find some bloody clothes? A bloody knife?" Connor smacked a fist in his palm. "Oh, wait. *We* have that."

"Maybe she has my button." Savannah crept toward the hallway leading to the rooms in the back. She paused at the only door that was closed, resting her fingertips on the handle and cocking her head. The hair on the back of her neck quivered for a second before she turned the doorknob.

She gulped when, out of nowhere, the cold barrel of a gun pressed against her temple.

Chapter Nine

The distinctive sound of a safety being released from a handgun cut through the air. Connor reached for his waistband, but he'd left his own weapon at home.

"Savannah!"

At his call, she came stumbling back into the room, a large bearded man prodding her forward at gunpoint.

"What the hell are you doing in my place?"

Connor's adrenaline whooshed and receded, leaving him dizzy. He clenched his hands at his sides. "*Your* place? This is Tiffany James's place, and we came up here to return her keys."

"A-and leave her a card." Savannah took a

small step away from the man holding her at gunpoint. "We just saw her at the pool, and I accidentally took her keys."

The man growled, "Why not just go back to the pool and give them to her?"

"She was going to get a massage. We didn't want to disturb her."

Savannah's demeanor had him in awe. She could think on her feet with the best of them.

"With Diego?" The bearded man's voice boomed behind her.

"What?" Savannah twisted her head around.

Connor held out his hand. "Put the gun away, man. This is a misunderstanding. We're not here to rip you off. Savannah came up here to leave Tiffany an attorney's card. Put the gun down."

The man secured his weapon and shoved it into the waistband of his ripped jeans. "You're Savannah Wedgewood, Niles's ex."

"That's right, and you are…?"

"Denny. Denny Cosgrove, Tiffany's…ex."

Connor's gaze tracked over Denny's tousled hair and bare chest. Didn't look like Denny and Tiffany were ex-anything.

"This is Connor." Savannah waved her hand at him.

At least she hadn't called *him* an ex.

Denny lunged forward with an outstretched paw and squeezed the hell out of Connor's hand. "Sorry about the gun. I thought someone had broken in."

"If we had thought anyone was here, we wouldn't have just waltzed in with the key." Savannah dangled Tiffany's key chain from her finger before dropping it on a table. "Sorry. We'll just leave this here."

"And that card?" Denny scratched his tattooed chest as he eyed Savannah.

"Of course." She dug in her purse and pulled out a card, wedging it beneath the key chain.

Denny slid the card toward him with one thick finger, squinting at the print. "Is this Niles's attorney? Is Tiffany getting something from Niles?"

"I believe so, yes." Savannah slid a quick

glance Connor's way. "Have the police talked to you yet?"

"Me?" Denny's face reddened. "Why should they talk to me? I got nothing to do with that murder. I never even met the guy."

"I mean when they talked to Tiffany. If you're staying here..."

"I'm not staying here. Just picking up some stuff Tif has of mine."

"Okay." Connor reached out and grabbed Savannah's hand. "We'll get out of your way."

Denny waved the card at them. "Thanks for this. Tif deserves something after what that guy put her through."

Once outside the stuffy condo, they marched toward Savannah's car in silence. Connor got in the passenger side and waited until Savannah was behind the wheel.

"That's why Tiffany didn't want us at her place. She's still hooking up with Denny and didn't want you to know."

"Denny sure seemed interested in Niles's money, didn't he?"

"Looks like Niles wasn't the only one stepping out in that relationship." Connor buzzed down his window as Savannah started the car. "And Denny is one dude you don't wanna cross."

"He *was* a little eager to pull out that gun."

"It's not just that, Savannah. Did you see his tattoos? He belongs to Sons of Chaos."

"The motorcycle gang? You knew that from his tattoos?"

"They're like any other gang. They get certain tattoos that mark their membership and standing in the organization."

"You think I should mention this to the police when I go in tomorrow to give my DNA?"

"Why not? They asked you before if you knew anyone who would want to kill Niles. Denny looks like a good suspect to me."

"Do you think Tiffany set up Niles? Maybe not for murder, but to fleece him?" Savannah maneuvered the car out of the parking lot of the condo complex and joined a stream of traffic.

"That could've been the plan, but you don't think Niles is that naive, do you?" Connor rubbed his chin, which had been itching ever since he saw Denny's full beard. "Maybe they were playing each other. He was getting what he wanted out of her and paying her for it."

Savannah wrinkled her nose. "That sounds so…tawdry. And if Niles was compensating Tiffany for her company, why would she want to kill the goose laying the golden eggs? Why would Denny?"

"Maybe they knew about the will and figured she'd get more with Niles dead—or at least get it as a lump sum and then she could be with Denny."

Savannah shook her head. "I can't imagine two men more different than Niles and Denny."

"Niles and I aren't exactly twins, either."

A rosy blush tinged her cheeks. "That was kind of the point."

"Because what we had was so bad?"

"Because I didn't need anyone or anything else reminding me of you after I left."

"Why?"

Savannah shifted in her seat and sighed, "If I couldn't have you, I didn't want to be thinking of you every day."

As the car idled at a red light, Connor brushed his knuckles down her forearm. "But you could've had me. Didn't I make that clear?"

"There was too much guilt for me, Connor." She sniffled. "My stepfather's associates killed your father because he was protecting my mom, and that strained your relationship with *your* mom."

"I always had an uncomfortable relationship with my mom. You know that."

"I'm sure all that happened between our families made it worse, and the fact that you sided with me over her."

"My father was doing his job. He was protecting a citizen of San Juan Beach."

"We both know he never would've been

there if my mom hadn't called him personally."

"If I can forgive you, why can't you forgive yourself? You don't even have anything to forgive. You were a barely out of your teens, still in college."

The knuckles on Savannah's hands turned white as she clenched the wheel. "I don't want to talk about this anymore, Connor."

He turned his head and stared at the passing scenery. Savannah's excuses didn't make sense. There had to be more. He'd accepted that she just wasn't that into him, but the heat between them still sizzled. What he wouldn't give to be a fly on the wall in her session with Thomas.

But now he had to settle for a fake relationship with the woman he loved more than anything, the woman he'd lie, cheat and steal for.

"Don't you think it would be a good idea if I dropped by the sheriff's department right now to give them my DNA? Would that make me seem more cooperative?"

"More anxious. They told you to come in tomorrow. If you keep your original appointment, that's cooperative enough."

Savannah flipped a U-turn and Connor clutched the armrest as the tires of the car squealed. "Where are you going?"

"The scene of the crime."

His fingernails dug into the leather of the armrest. "Are you kidding?"

"House is still in my name. I still have keys. Why not?"

"Because your ex was just murdered there and you're a suspect. It might look suspicious."

"If someone sees me. Will the cops have someone watching the place?"

"Probably not. I'm sure they're done processing the crime scene by now. They've taken their prints, their pictures, their evidence."

"Which apparently does *not* include the button from my blouse."

"Too bad we didn't have a chance to look for that at Tiffany's." Connor rolled his tight shoulders. They had too much to deal with too fast.

As Savannah drove through the pristine neighborhood of La Jolla, Connor glanced at her profile. "Are you sure you want to do this?"

"If we're going to conduct our own investigation into Niles's murder, we have to start with the scene of the crime."

"What do you think you'll find there?"

Her head whipped around. "Why are you trying to dissuade me? You said yourself the sheriff's department has processed the crime scene. My name is still on the title of that house, I have the keys and I have every right to go there. What's the problem?"

Connor rubbed his jaw. What *was* the problem? The nagging voice in the back of his brain that kept telling him the killer would want to return to the scene of the crime?

"Don't want it to look bad for you." He lifted one shoulder.

Reaching across the console, she rubbed his thigh. "Thanks, but if there's nobody there to see me, that's not going to happen. Besides, I have a reason to be there."

"Which is?" He held his breath.

"Niles worked from home a lot, and he has company files there. I want them."

"The homicide detectives would've taken his laptop and any other devices at the house."

"I'm talking about paper files—like the ones he was supposed to hand over to me that night before we were both incapacitated."

"Okay, that's your story. Stick to it."

She huffed out a breath. "It's not a story, Connor. I swear, sometimes you act like I'm guilty."

"We don't know what happened that night, Savannah. You…blacked out."

"Sometimes you act like I'm guilty—and that I *know* I'm guilty."

Connor stared out the window as the rolling green lawns and lush, colorful landscaping rushed by. "Did you like living here?"

She huffed out a long sigh. "I did. The house is beautiful."

"If you're still on the title, that means the house is yours, too, right?"

Silence descended in the car as Savannah maneuvered the winding roads uphill, hunching forward in her seat. The hard set of her jaw told him she had no intention of answering his question, even though he knew the answer. With Niles's death, she stood to gain control of Snap App, millions in life insurance money and a multimillion-dollar home in La Jolla. Quite a haul.

"It's right around the next curve." She swung the wheel and slowed the car. "And I don't see any cop cars out front."

Even if he hadn't seen pictures of the house before, the yellow crime scene tape stirring in the ocean breeze was a dead giveaway. The white Mediterranean loomed at the end of the cul-de-sac, and Connor knew the Pacific roiled and scrambled over the rocks just beyond and downhill from the house.

How the hell had Savannah sneaked out of here on foot and walked home?

She pulled into the driveway and cut the engine. "The walk home wasn't bad, especially after I kicked off my heels."

Before he had a chance to answer, she hopped out of the car and slammed the door. By the time he scrambled from the car and had followed her up the walkway, she was yanking yellow tape from the front door.

She dangled it in front of her from her fingertips. "Does this mean they plan to come back?"

"Not necessarily." He snatched the tape from her hand and crumpled it in his fist. "The cops are not going to clean up a murder scene for you. They leave that chore to you."

"I remember." With her mouth tight, she shoved her key into the lock and pushed open the door.

Of course, Savannah and her mother had had to take care of the mess when his father shot and killed Manny in their home. Dad had even taken care of that for Georgie, calling in a cleaning crew from San Diego that specialized in crime scene cleanup; blood, brains, tissue—they did it all. What would Savannah and he find here?

As he stepped over the threshold of the house she used to share with her husband, Connor tilted back his head to take in the vaulted ceiling above the foyer, and squinted into the light. The blue, green and white furnishings that littered the great room looked like a continuation of the ocean and sand at the foot of the cliffs over which the big house loomed. He could see Savannah's stamp on the room—bright, airy and carefree. What secrets lurked beneath this cheery facade?

She shot him a look from beneath her dark lashes. "Do you like it?"

"It's…beachy."

"Appropriately so." She crossed the room to the staircase and put one foot on the bottom step, resting her hand on the banister. "D-do you want to go upstairs and see it?"

"Might as well get it over with." He pulled in a deep breath and blew it out as he took

Savannah's hand and marched up the stairs ahead of her.

When they hit the second level, she squeezed his hand and said, "Last room at the end of the hall."

The door to the master bedroom gaped open, one band of yellow tape across the opening. Connor ducked beneath it and crossed into the room, tripping to a stop when he saw the bloodstain on the throw rug that carried over to the hardwood floor.

He whistled. "Niles lost a lot of blood."

"I know."

"Take me through what you remember." He skirted the mess on the floor and sauntered to the French doors that led to a balcony and a magnificent view of the Pacific.

He unlocked one of the doors and swung it open. The white drapes unfurled into the room, caught on a sudden sea breeze.

Savannah had got hung up at the room's entrance, her eyes wide and shimmering pools. "I—I woke up on that side of the bed, the same side as Nile's body on the floor."

She took a stuttering step into the room. As she shuffled around the bed, her sandals scuffing against the polished wood, her gaze darted to the place where she'd found her ex-husband, his flesh punctured and ripped by a knife—the same one hidden on Connor's property.

She thrust a finger at the tousled bed. "There. I woke up there, naked, cuts on my right hand. My mouth dry as a cotton ball, my brain foggy, confused."

"Was the door to the balcony closed and the drapes drawn?"

"No. Just like now, there was a breeze that morning, and the door was slightly ajar. I was dreaming that I was in the water and struggling for the surface."

"Did you see Niles right away?"

"I didn't see Niles at all at first. It was still dark outside and the room was dark. I—I stubbed my toe on his body." She hugged herself, and dug her fingers into the flesh of her upper arms. "When I flicked on the light, I saw him at my feet."

Connor tilted his head. "Weren't you afraid the killer might still be in the house?"

"I don't know why, but that never occurred to me." She tossed back her hair. "I guess I figured he'd committed the act and taken off."

Connor pulled the rest of the story out of her in bits and pieces. It hadn't changed much from the account she'd given him from the moment she'd landed on his doorstep.

She showed him where she'd found her button and how she'd stuffed it into the pocket of her slacks.

"I guess I missed my pocket and that's how Letty found the button, or it fell out when I finished tidying up."

"Where did you go after you…cleaned up the room?"

"Down to Niles's office." She pulled her light sweater around her body. "I wanted the file Niles had promised me."

"Must've been an important file for you to think about it in a moment of panic."

Her eyes narrowed briefly like a cat's that

had considered and then dismissed some prey. "That's why Niles and I got together. That's why I came to this house. I wasn't going to leave it behind." She crooked her index finger. "I'll show you."

Once again Connor ducked beneath the yellow tape crisscrossed over the door. He followed Savannah down the curved staircase, her composure causing a tickle on the back of his neck.

The sight of Niles's blood had shaken her, but if he thought Savannah was going to collapse against his chest in a fit of despair, he'd be dead wrong. She'd been oddly stoic after Manny's death, too.

She strode across the great room and pushed open a door that led to an office, its walls lined with bookshelves, a single large window framing a profusion of color in the front garden.

"We must've had a drink." Savannah flicked her fingers toward the wet bar. "There were two glasses over there, a lipstick stain on one of them."

He drew his brows over his nose. "Is that something you'd do normally?"

"To tell you the truth, not really, especially if I'd already had a drink. But if Niles was insisting, I might do it to appease him, just to get my hands on the file."

"Maybe it wasn't your drink."

"Too late now. I dumped the booze in the sink and rinsed out those glasses."

"What kind of booze?"

She swooped down on the wet bar and tapped a cut glass crystal bottle with her fingernail. "This scotch. It was Niles's favorite."

"Maybe we need to take that with us, see what's in it. If you think both you and Niles might've been drugged, maybe that's the source."

"Good idea." She grabbed the bottle from the shelf and put it on the edge of the wet bar. "So, I came in here, grabbed the file and hiked down the hill and through the backstreets to my house."

"The file was on the desk?"

"No." She raised a finger. "Which was

weird. There's a false bottom in one of the desk drawers and the file was still there."

"How'd you know it would be there?"

"I'm pretty sure Niles told me on the way over. We often put important papers in there, papers we might not want to secure in the safe but didn't want out in the open."

"What was in this file?"

"Financials. Stuff we don't want to reveal to the general public. I didn't think it was out of the ordinary for the file to be there."

"You just said it was weird that the file was there."

"That the file was *still* there." She shook her purse off her shoulder and unzipped it. "Whatever happened to us must've happened pretty fast if Niles didn't even have time to remove the file from the desk drawer. When I came down here, I expected the file to be on the desk. When it wasn't, I knew he hadn't taken it out of the drawer yet, and I was able to retrieve it from its hiding place."

"What are you doing now?"

Savannah had moved behind the mahogany desk, holding up a pen she'd pulled from her purse. "I'll show you how it works."

Connor joined her behind the desk, crouching next to her as she pulled open the bottom drawer on the left side.

She shoved aside some hanging folders and inserted the tip of the pen into a minuscule hole in the bottom of the drawer. As Savannah wiggled the pen, her tongue lodged in the corner of her mouth, Connor heard a small *click*.

She lifted a panel from the bottom of the drawer, exposing a cavity that held a few file folders and a flash drive. "I took the file from here."

"Handy. I wonder why he didn't take it out when you got back here."

"I can't tell you. I don't remember." She replaced the panel and sat back on her heels.

Connor leaned over her, grabbed the pen and scooted the files back into place. As he set the pen on the desk the top sprang free and rolled off the edge. "Looks like you broke your..."

Connor's throat tightened as he eyed the various pieces.

"That's okay. I don't even know where I got that pen. Must be one of Niles's."

Connor prodded the broken pen with his knuckle and then brushed if off the table and crushed it beneath the heel of his shoe.

Savannah's eyes widened. "What the hell are you doing?"

"That might be a pen, but it's doubling as a recording device."

Chapter Ten

Savannah choked and scrambled backward like a crab, away from the shards of pen littering the Persian rug. "A—a recording device? Someone's been listening to me? To us?"

"Or tracking your movements." He stirred the pieces with the toe of his shoe. "It could be a GPS or even a camera. I can't tell, but if the eavesdropper was still listening I don't think we gave it away that we knew what it was. The pen rolled off the table and broke. That's all he knows."

"Oh, God." Savannah clutched her throat with one hand. "It must've been in my purse from the beginning. Someone planted it when I was here, in this house."

The sound of a car door slamming had the two of them locking eyes.

"Now what?" Still on the floor, Savannah crawled to the window and hooked her finger on the edge of the drapes, peering outside. "Damn."

"The cops?" Connor dropped to his knees and scooped up the pieces of the pen or microphone or GPS or whatever it was into his palm.

"Niles's sister, Melanie."

"Does she have a key?"

"I'm sure she does, or she wouldn't be here." Savannah jumped to her feet and scurried out of the room, calling over her shoulder, "Act naturally."

She hit the foyer just as Melanie pushed open the front door.

Niles's sister jerked back, releasing the door, which swung open and hit the wall. "Savannah, you scared the hell out of me.

I saw the car but I thought it was one of Niles's."

"You gave me a fright, too." Savannah descended on Melanie and wrapped her arms around her former sister-in-law's thin frame. "I'm so sorry about Niles."

Melanie returned the hug. "Thank you. It was awful news. Who'd want to kill my brother? Do you think you're in danger, too?"

Oh, yeah. She was in danger. "I have no idea who'd want to kill Niles, but I hope to God I'm not on anyone's list."

Melanie cocked her head. "Really? Who are we fooling? Niles had made some enemies since you two struck it rich."

Connor's flip-flops slapped the floor behind Savannah, and she made a half turn. "Melanie Wedgewood, this is Connor Wells. Connor, Niles's sister, Melanie."

"Nice to meet you, and I'm sorry for your loss." Connor reached around Savannah to shake Melanie's hand.

"Pretty crazy stuff. You never think murder is going to hit your family." Melanie smoothed her short dark hair back from her forehead with one hand. "But here we are."

"What *are* you doing here?" Savannah shoved an unsteady hand in the pocket of her sweater. She hadn't yet recovered from Connor's discovery about the pen, but in a way it wasn't the worst news she'd had all day. Now maybe Connor would believe that someone was trying to set her up, instead of shooting doubt at her from his impossibly blue eyes.

Melanie jabbed a finger in Savannah's direction. "You may have inherited everything Niles had, but I'm still his next of kin and the cops told me I was basically responsible for Niles's funeral…and other things."

"Don't go up there." Savannah put a hand on Melanie's arm. "You don't need to see that. Connor knows about these things, people you can hire."

"Really?" Melanie's heavily lined eyes widened. "I was shocked when the sheriff's department told me they didn't clean up the…mess left behind in a homicide."

"There are companies that will take care of that. I'll look some up for you right now, if you two want to talk privately," Connor offered.

"I don't think Savannah and I have anything to discuss in secret, do we?" Melanie arched an eyebrow in her direction. "But if you want to help me out, I'd appreciate it. I wouldn't even know where to start looking."

Connor held up his cell phone. "I got it."

As he wandered back to Niles's office, Melanie jerked her thumb in his direction. "Dreamboat, if I actually swung that way."

"Speaking of dreamboats, is Faye with you?"

"She had clients she couldn't leave. She never liked Niles anyway."

"She would be here for you, not Niles."

"I never liked Niles much, either, at least not lately." Melanie put a hand over her mouth. "I didn't just say that. I'm a terrible person and an awful sister."

Savannah squeezed Melanie's shoulder. "We all say things during times of stress.

I know you loved Niles, even when he was being impossible."

"He messed up." Melanie brushed a tear from her cheek. "He should've treated you better. Maybe should've treated other people better, as well."

"I don't think that would've changed anything, Melanie. We just weren't meant to be a romantic couple. We should've just stayed business partners."

"That would've never worked for Niles. He was smitten with you, although I never got the impression the smit was mutual." Melanie's gaze tracked to the office door, which Connor had closed behind him.

Savannah spun around, flinging her arms out to her sides. "Now it's all a big mess—Niles dead, murdered. I know he had his enemies, but I can't think of anyone who'd want him dead."

"What about that girlfriend of his?" Melanie swept past Savannah and meandered to the sliding glass doors that led to the backyard. "Tiffany. From what I could tell, she was kind of a shady character. Who dates someone you meet while she's dancing around a pole?"

"Niles and lots of other men." Savannah folded her arms and perched on the arm of her favorite recliner. "I can't see Tiffany murdering Niles. She'd be killing her benefactor…"

"But?"

"But what?" Savannah lifted her chin and met Melanie's eyes.

"That sentence had a definite *but* at the end of it."

Savannah raised and dropped her shoulders. "Looks like Tiffany has an ex hanging around—a scary-looking biker dude."

"Maybe that's it." Melanie snapped her fingers. "Jealous biker dude."

"I'll make sure I mention him to the detectives."

"You haven't spoken to them yet?" Melanie narrowed her dark eyes, looking enough like Niles to give Savannah the chills.

"Yes, they came down to San Juan Beach—

where I've been staying with Connor—to question me, but they want me to stop by the station so I can give up my DNA and to ask more questions. I'm going in tomorrow."

"Your DNA?" Melanie clicked her tongue. "They don't suspect you, do they?"

"Ex-wife getting control of the multimillion-dollar company, life insurance money, house in La Jolla." Savannah jabbed a finger into her chest. "Number one suspect right here."

Melanie snorted, "Ridiculous. They can ask me. Besides, weren't you with dreamboat in there at the time of the murder?"

"How do you know that?"

"Uh, I asked the detectives." She raised her hand. "Not that I suspected you."

"I was with Connor."

"Done deal." Melanie brushed her hands together.

Connor exited the office, tilting his phone back and forth in front of him. "Called a company for you, and they're coming out tomorrow, unless that doesn't work."

"You *are* a dreamboat." Melanie blew a kiss in Connor's direction. "Thank you so much."

"While you're here, you're welcome to take anything, Melanie." Savannah waved her hand around the room. "Niles has some family pics and some things from your parents."

"Wow." Melanie blinked her eyes and dabbed at the corners. "It's just my brother Newland and I now in our immediate family, and Newland's no use while he's battling his demons. That hurts."

Savannah wrapped Melanie in another hug. "Take as much time as you need here. Are you talking to the detectives while you're in San Diego?"

"I spoke with them on the phone, but they wanted me to come in for another interview, a face-to-face." She sniffed and shook her finger at Savannah. "And you'd better believe I'm going to tell them you had nothing to do with Niles's death."

"I appreciate it. Give my love to Faye."

"I will. She'll be sorry she missed you." Melanie wedged a hand on her hip. "I'm not driving you two away, am I?"

"We were just leaving when you arrived." Connor pointed at the door. "But you ladies can have a few more minutes. I'm going to get that bag from the car, Savannah, and pack up a few of those files you wanted from Niles's office."

"Okay." Savannah watched Connor leave with a furrow between her eyebrows. Files? Maybe he meant that bottle of scotch. Melanie wouldn't miss that, as she was a recovering alcoholic. Niles was the only Wedgewood sibling who had escaped that scourge.

She and Melanie chatted for a few more minutes until Connor returned with an empty gym bag hitched over his shoulder.

"I'll be done in a minute."

By the time he emerged from the office, Savannah and Melanie had said their good-byes and Savannah joined Connor at the front door.

"Keep me posted on the funeral plans, Melanie."

"I will. I know I'll have to wait until they release Niles's body." Melanie closed her eyes and clutched her hands in front of her.

Savannah asked, "You sure you'll be okay here by yourself?"

"Killer's not coming back, is he?"

As they stepped down the front porch, Connor whispered in Savannah's ear, "I wish he would so we could wrap this up."

"What's in the bag?" Savannah pinged the side of the black canvas with her fingernail.

"That scotch, the pieces of the broken pen and the rest of that stuff from the false-bottom drawer." He hugged the bag to his chest. "You never know."

As they wound down the hill, Savannah glanced at Connor. "Someone was following me or listening to me with that pen."

"Or both. I'm not sure what kind of device it is. I just know it's not a pen, or at least it's more than a pen."

"If someone was listening to me, they

could've heard my conversation with Letty. Could've shown up early to kill her and take that button."

"The person listening in also knows exactly our train of thought, knows we went to see Tiffany, knows we were at the house. I can't even think of what else."

"B-but it definitely looks like someone is trying to set me up, right? That pen must've been planted in my purse the night of Niles's murder. I've never seen it before." She pressed a hand to her forehead. "I haven't been imagining this, and that same person put the knife in my car and tried to steer the detectives toward it."

She slid one hand from the steering wheel and pressed it against her fluttering belly. "That means he knows where I live, somehow broke into my car and stashed that knife in my trunk."

"Or he broke into your house, got your car keys and used them to get into your car. Did you have your keys with you that night, even though you'd left your car at home?"

"I didn't."

"How'd you get into your house when you got home?"

"Used the code on my garage door to get in that way. I always leave the door from my laundry room to the garage open."

"Bad idea."

She rolled her eyes. "That's a moot point now. Someone set me up for Niles's murder, but why? Why take out both of us by killing him and framing me?"

"Who stands to gain with both of you out of the picture? Who gets the company?"

"My mom is beneficiary for almost everything I have. As…unconventional as my mother is, I don't think she'd be killing Niles and framing me for his murder."

"And Niles's share?"

"His sister."

"Melanie?"

She poked his thigh. "No way. Melanie doesn't even care that much about money."

"Her boyfriend? Spouse?"

"Wife. Faye has a great career as an attorney with a big firm in San Francisco. They're set, happy. They're not interested in what Niles has, especially since Melanie saw how much wealth changed her brother—and not for the better."

"Maybe money isn't the motive. Is there someone at the company who hates the two of you? Disgruntled employee?"

Savannah sucked in her bottom lip and squinted at the road. "There was a guy, Brian Donahue. We had to let him go. He was in charge of quality-assurance testing and couldn't get along with anyone. He threatened to destroy code and we had him escorted out of the building and off the premises."

"How long ago was this?"

"Three or four months."

"Did he threaten either of you?"

"On his way out of the building? Hell, yes."

"You need to mention his name to the detectives tomorrow."

"There's a lot I could tell them tomorrow, but half of it would implicate me, so I'd better keep my mouth shut." She flipped down her visor. "I wonder if anyone has discovered Letty's body yet."

"I'm sure you'll find out tomorrow when you go in for questioning." Connor rubbed the back of his neck. "Don't you ever eat? I'm starving."

"I suppose I could force down some food. Should we stop on the way back to your place or wait until we get to San Juan?"

"If you can hold out for another twenty minutes, let's wait. I think you should show your face around town a little more, get people used to seeing you there. I also want to find out if there's any news about the fire. Now that we found that pen, there's a very real possibility someone followed you out to my place and set fire to that shed for some reason."

"To smoke out the knife. Someone could've been watching you when you went outside to hide it."

"I wasn't waving it around when I went to the storage shed."

"The person could've just made the assumption, or even verified the assumption when we left for lunch."

"I'm not dismissing the idea. That's why I want to keep my ear to the ground in San Juan for any news."

By the time they rolled into San Juan, Savannah's stomach was rumbling with hunger. This time Connor did direct her to one of their old haunts—a funky beach hut with plastic tables and chairs spilling onto the sand.

When Savannah stepped out of the car, she stretched her arms over her head, interlocking her fingers as the ocean breeze toyed with the ends of her hair. She took a deep breath of the salty air and forgot about Niles, Letty, the blackout…all of it. At least it had all led back to this town and this man—at least for a few weeks. Months?

The beach spell must've cast itself over Connor, too. He laced his fingers through hers and tugged her toward the café.

The morning surfers had long cleared out and the restaurant wasn't open for dinner, so a straggling late-lunch crowd greeted them as they walked through the door.

The waitress waved her hand around the small room. "Sit anywhere you like."

"We're going to head out to the sand."

Keeping hold of Savannah's hand, Connor led her past the tables inside to the ones nestled in the dry sand beyond.

Savannah plopped down in the plastic chair while Connor adjusted the umbrella to ward off the afternoon sun. She kicked off her sandals and dug her toes into the sand. "What a morning. Do you think it was productive?"

"I do." Connor leaned back in his chair and rested one ankle on his other knee. "We know that Tiffany had her ex on the side while she was engaged to Niles, and that her ex is an imposing guy with a gun."

"Niles was stabbed."

"I remember, but Denny could've used the gun to intimidate Niles. He also has his motorcycle gang connections."

"Can I get you something to drink?" the young waitress called from the edge of the patio, not willing to make the trek across the sand.

Savannah called back, "Iced tea."

"Make it two." Connor held up two fingers in the air. "We also got that scotch from Niles's wet bar that one or both of you had probably been drinking that night. If you think you were drugged, we can get a test run on that."

"Now we have the knife and the scotch." Savannah wedged an elbow on the table and sank her chin into her palm. "How are we going to get those tested?"

"I have a friend who's a PI and he has friends and they have friends. I know he'll do this for me. I worked with him on a few cases when I was a cop. He's a good buddy. I can count on him."

"Without asking questions?"

"He trusts me, and I've done a few favors for him in the past—not that I have to bring those up."

"Like I did." Savannah stirred the sand with her toe.

"You were just using some insurance. I don't hold that against you." Connor brushed his thumb across her inner wrist. "I don't hold anything against you, Savannah."

She blinked behind her sunglasses. He had lots to blame her for—if he knew the truth.

The waitress had sent a busboy out to their table with the drinks, and he plodded across the sand, holding one in each hand.

Savannah broke away from Connor and smiled at the busboy. "Can you tell the waitress that we're ready to order?"

Before he could answer, a woman shrieked behind him and traipsed across the patio. "I heard you were back in town."

Savannah jumped up from her chair and hugged her friend Jamie. "In the flesh."

Jamie squeezed her in return and then punched Connor in the shoulder. "You could've told us you two were back together."

Connor smirked. "I didn't want to jinx anything."

Jamie waved her hands at the busboy. "I'll

take their order, and you can tell that lazy Annie she can stick to the tables inside."

She turned back to Savannah. "I was so glad to hear you were back in SJB, but I'm sorry about your ex." Jamie curled a hand around her throat. "That's terrible."

"Awful. I still can't quite believe it happened." Savannah grabbed her drink and plunged a straw into the liquid. "I hope the police catch the guy who did it."

"I know. So creepy." Jamie reached into her rear pocket and whipped out a notebook. "I'm sorry it's taken so long to get your order. I figure if you don't want to walk in dry sand, you shouldn't work at a beach café."

"I'll have the grilled chicken sandwich with fries."

"And I'll have the cheeseburger with fries." Connor tucked the small plastic menus into the menu holder on the table. "Jamie, have you heard anything about Jimmy Takata setting that fire at my place yesterday?"

"I did hear some rumors, but I don't know

if the cops have talked to him yet. I wouldn't put that past Jimmy or any of the Cove Boys. They're out of control. Think they own this town." She aimed her pencil at Connor. "It's not the same without your dad and the San Juan PD."

"Thanks, Jamie."

As she walked away, Connor pulled out his phone.

"Who are you calling?"

"I forgot to call the sheriff's department to give them the tip about Jimmy."

While Connor was on the phone, Savannah looked through her text messages and a few emails. Her battery was already down to 30 percent and she'd barely used the phone all day, but she had no intention of replacing it now. If the police asked her about her cell tomorrow, she wanted to be able to show them the broken one.

"That's done." Connor snapped the phone on the table. "They'd already heard a few things about Jimmy, and when I told them what happened yesterday morning at the beach, they thought it was important enough to question him."

"Maybe Jimmy did set fire to that storage shed, but it doesn't change the fact that someone planted a pen in my purse to track my movements or conversations or both."

Connor raised an eyebrow. "Anything else unusual in your purse?"

"No, I checked."

Several minutes later, Jamie delivered their food, and they both ate as if it were their first meal in several days.

Investigating had definitely improved her appetite, Savannah thought. It beat sitting around waiting for stuff to happen—like an arrest.

On their way out of the restaurant, they chatted with Jamie and her husband, and then walked to the car for the drive to Connor's place.

Savannah dangled the keys. "You mind driving?"

Snatching the key chain from her hand, Connor opened the passenger door for her.

Savannah tipped her head back against the headrest, closing her eyes. "I can't take any more today and it's not even dinnertime."

"You have another big day tomorrow."

"I know—that police interview."

"And your appointment with Thomas."

"Yeah, and that." She opened one eye. "You know you can't sit in with me, right?"

He snorted, "I don't want that. I'm just hoping he can help you with the blackout. Help you with some memories."

I don't want to remember.

Savannah closed her eye again and settled her shoulders against the car seat.

When Connor pulled onto the road leading to his property, a sigh escaped Savannah's lips. Her second day here and it already felt like coming home. What would it be like to stay here forever? She could run the company from here, go into the office once a week.

By the time Connor parked, her foolish dreams had seeped away. The more time she spent with Connor, the more uncomfortable it was keeping the truth from him. She'd either have to spill the beans or she'd have to leave him…again.

She struggled to get out of the car on her heavy limbs. She wanted to lie down, curl up and sleep for a thousand hours, or at least until she could put all this mess behind her.

"Are you okay?" Connor had come around to the passenger side after retrieving his gym bag from the back seat and slinging it over his shoulder. He ran his hands down her arms. "Your eyes look heavy."

"The food and the sun made me sleepy."

"Take a nap. We have nothing to do, unless you have Snap App business. I'm going to make a few calls."

"The only business going on at Snap App right now is gossip. I do want to call a meeting for later this week, though, and give the troops a pep talk."

"Then go to sleep. You need it." He took her arm and they walked up the two steps to the porch together.

Connor shoved the key in the dead bolt and

cocked his head. "I thought I locked this before we left."

He removed the key from the top lock and inserted it into the one on the door handle. "At least this one's locked."

He pushed open the door and held his hand behind him. "Wait a minute."

Savannah's heart rate picked up. "What's wrong?"

"Give me a minute to look around."

She balled up the sweater in her hands and hugged it to her chest as she watched Connor walk into the hallway.

He disappeared for several minutes and then called out to her, "It's all right. Everything looks fine."

Savannah's shoulders sagged and she tripped over the threshold, slamming the front door behind her. "Don't scare me like that. What was the problem?"

"Thought I locked that dead bolt. I always do."

"I'm throwing you off your routine." She tossed her purse onto the nearest chair. "Are you going to call your PI buddy to get the blood on that knife tested and have him look at the scotch?"

"I sure am. Are you going to take that nap?"

"I feel like I could sleep forever right now." She shuffled into the kitchen. "I'm going to get some water and lie down."

She reached into the cupboard above the dishwasher and grabbed a glass. "You want some?"

"I'm good." Connor sat on the couch and kicked his feet onto the coffee table, his phone in one hand.

Savannah dispensed some water from the refrigerator and wedged one hip against the counter. As she took a sip from the glass, her gaze scanned the countertop where her phone charger cord lay coiled in a circle.

She frowned. Connor must've unplugged it. She always left it in the outlet, as she needed to constantly charge her stupid phone—like now.

She shoved off the counter and then gasped.

Spinning back around, she gripped the edge of the counter and gulped. She swept her hands across the smooth granite, pushing Connor's bills and mail to the floor.

"What are you doing over there?"

She flattened her hands on the cool surface and hunched forward. "My file is gone. Someone broke in here and stole that file folder."

Chapter Eleven

"I knew it." Connor sprang from the couch like a jack-in-the-box and ate up the distance between them in two steps. "Where was it?"

Savannah slapped the counter with her palm. "Here. I left it right here. When I charged my phone, I was putting it on top of the file folder."

"You're sure?" Even as the words left his mouth, he realized their stupidity. The look on Savannah's face told him she was sure.

She plucked at the phone charger and wrapped it around her finger. "I noticed this first. I always leave my charger plugged in. You didn't unplug it, did you?"

"No." Connor swiveled his head, his gaze

darting about the room. "He or she was careful. When the lock tipped me off, I looked around carefully and didn't see anything out of place."

"The knife." Savannah's violet eyes darkened, or maybe they just looked dark set against her white face. "Where's the knife?"

"Why would he take the knife? If he is trying to set you up, he'd want to leave that with you."

"But if he located it, he might call those detectives again and give them a hot tip—just like he did about the trunk of my car. We both know that's why they looked in my trunk."

"Stay here." Connor ran outside, letting the screen door bang behind him. He circled around to the back of the house and charged toward one of two oak trees where a hammock usually hung. He plunged his hand into the hole in the trunk, his fingers twisting around the plastic bag. He dragged it out and carried it back to the house.

"This is becoming a game of hide the

bloody knife." He dropped it on his fireplace mantel. "Anything else missing? Your laptop?"

Savannah flew out of the kitchen and down the hallway. Several seconds later she popped her head around the corner of the hallway. "It's there. Too bad he didn't take it. That, at least, I could've tracked. That file is gone forever."

"Why was that set of data in hard copy instead of online?"

"I couldn't tell you. I originally tried to look it up and when I couldn't find it online, I asked Niles, and that's when he told me he'd printed it out and had a hard copy of it."

"Why did you want to see it?"

"I was surprised by our quarterly earnings and had been going through the different departments to double-check the figures. I couldn't find this one department's. Niles didn't explain why he had it separate."

"Could Niles have been cooking the books?"

"Niles?" Savannah drove two fingers into her temple. "I doubt it. Why would he? It's not like the company wasn't doing well—isn't doing well."

Connor walked into the living room and snagged the strap of the gym bag. He swung it onto a kitchen stool and unzipped the side pocket. He gathered the pieces of the broken pen and dumped them on the counter.

"I now know this pen was a listening device. How else would the intruder have known you had this file? He heard you talking about it and wanted it."

"Oh, my God. Why?" Savannah placed her hand on her forehead. "My head's spinning. I don't understand why anyone would want that file."

"Whoever took it just tipped his hand. Once you figure out why the file is so important, it'll lead you to Niles's killer."

"By then, the killer will have destroyed the file and any evidence it contains."

"You can't get that data online? It must've existed online at some point. You're the computer genius, not me, but there has to be a way to recover it."

"I'll get on that when I go into the office for this meeting. In fact, I'm going to schedule that meeting right now by sending out a company-wide email."

"After your nap?" He raised one eyebrow.

"I'm wide-awake now."

"And it looks like I have another call to make before asking my friend to run a few tests for me."

"What call would that be?"

"Security system. I'm getting cameras installed—arson, burglary. What next?"

Clenching her teeth, Savannah raised her shoulders to her ears. "I don't want to think about what's next."

"What's next for you is setting up that meeting and then taking a nap. You look run-down."

"Do I?" She ran her hands over her face, still beautiful even with dark circles beneath her eyes and tension in every muscle.

"Tired." He touched the end of her nose with his fingertip, even though he wanted to do much more than that.

She blushed and coughed. "I'm going to grab my laptop, compose and send out that email and then curl up like a cat."

She slid from the kitchen stool, and he grabbed his phone and parked himself on one end of the couch. He had someone in mind already to set up the security system. He'd been planning to have one installed for the winery anyway. It just got fast-tracked.

His head jerked to the side when Savannah sat next to him and took his hand.

"You believe me now, don't you, Connor?" She squeezed his fingers. "You believe that I didn't kill Niles—in self-defense or otherwise? You believe that someone is trying to set me up?"

Curling his other hand around the back of her neck, he drew her close and touched his forehead to hers. "I do—the knife, the pen, the break-in."

"I—I mean it's clear that someone's trying to set me up, right?"

"It looks that way." Her lips were so close to his he could feel their warmth.

She broke away from him on a sigh. "You don't know how much I needed to hear that."

He raised a finger. "That doesn't mean I don't want you to still see Thomas tomorrow. If you can remember what happened at Niles's, it might help to ID his killer."

"I'm fine with seeing Thomas." She pushed up from the couch. "Looking forward to it, actually."

Through narrowed eyes, he watched her disappear down the hallway to get her laptop.

That was a lie. She was looking forward to seeing Thomas about as much as he'd be looking forward to a root canal. What other lies did she have on the tip of her tongue?

There was definitely something she wasn't telling him. This smelled like a setup all right, but who was setting up whom?

EARLY THAT EVENING, after Savannah had scheduled her meeting and taken a nap, she joined Connor on the floor in front of the TV and a pizza box.

She crossed her legs beneath her and

grabbed a paper plate. "You got all your stuff done?"

Connor held up a hand and ticked off one finger at a time. "Set up an appointment to get a security system installed. Contacted A.J. about testing the blood on the knife and the bottle of scotch. Hid the knife in a different spot and did some winery work. Just a typical day."

Savannah nudged his foot with her toes and held up a slice with cheese hanging off the edge. "Vinny's is still the best pizza in town."

"It is, and I didn't even need to consult you to know you'd want the pepperoni and Italian sausage—despite your vow to cut red meat from your diet. Now is not the time to stick to diets…or any other resolutions." He held up the bottle of red wine. "Another glass?"

"Just a half for me." She raised her index finger and thumb to give him the measurement and he dumped in a little more.

So much for those other resolutions.

"A.J. told me he knows a guy who can test that scotch for any added substances."

"And the knife?"

"He's working on it. That one's a little harder."

"No kidding." She swirled the ruby liquid in her glass.

"You look better already after that nap." He cocked his head and his blue eyes did a quick inventory of her features.

She didn't tell him that his admission that he believed she wasn't responsible for Niles's death went a long way to lifting the burden she carried on her shoulders. One burden down, one to go.

"I needed the rest. Now I need this pizza." She bit into the corner of the slice, the spiciness of the pepperoni exploding on her tongue.

"Any blowback from the meeting you called?"

"No, several members of upper management responded with their support. I can count on Nick Fresco and Lucy Shepherd and Hector Villalobos to have my back—Dee Dee, too. She was Niles's right hand... and his left, come to think of it."

"Would Dee Dee know about that file?"

"Maybe." Savannah dropped some crust on her plate and wiped her greasy fingers on a napkin. "I think I can ask her about it discreetly."

"Be careful while you're there, Savannah. This could all be work-related. Maybe you were supposed to die along with Niles."

"Thanks." She dusted the pizza crumbs from her fingertips and took a swig of wine. "That's just what I needed to hear. Someone's either trying to set me up for a murder I did not commit, or they're gonna kill me."

He pinched her knee. "Not while I'm around."

"Do you want to come to the office with me day after tomorrow?"

"I'll be there if you want."

"I want." She tore off another piece of pizza. "You can even accompany me to

Thomas's office tomorrow, if you promise to wait outside."

"Savannah, Thomas is a professional. What goes on between the two of you is strictly confidential." Connor put the wineglass to his lips and then pulled it away. "Makes me wonder, though."

"Wonder what?"

"Why you're so nervous."

"Oh, I don't know." She dropped the pizza slice. "We're both lying about where I was the night my ex-husband was murdered. I think I have a little to worry about."

"We'll get through this."

"Sometimes I feel like I can get through anything as long as I have you by my side." She cupped his strong jaw with her palm, the bristle from his five o'clock shadow tickling her skin.

"You only feel like that *sometimes*?" He twisted his head to the side and pressed a kiss against her palm. "I know having you here can make anything better, but you're not here, are you? Even when you're here, you're a million miles away. Be here. With me now."

Her eyes blurred with tears and Connor's face swam before her eyes. She couldn't love this man any more than she already did, but she could show him how much even if she couldn't tell him.

Curling her arms around his neck, she pressed her cheek against his and inhaled his masculine scent—mixed with pepperoni and red wine.

He plowed one hand into her hair and tugged back her head. He slanted his mouth across hers and caressed her lips in a soft, spicy kiss.

She answered with a sigh. She'd been waiting for that kiss ever since she'd thrown herself at him in his driveway, her hopes and her anxiety level high. And he'd helped her in every way, despite breaking the law, putting himself in jeopardy and not quite believing in her.

He pulled her against him in an awkward embrace, but really, nothing was ever awkward between them. They were made for each other.

She settled into his lap, hanging on with an arm wrapped around his waist, and he finished that kiss, pressing his lips against hers, invading her mouth with his tongue.

She toyed with his tongue as she slid her hands beneath his T-shirt and smoothed her fingertips across the muscles of his defined chest. "Your body is as perfect as I remember."

"And yours—" he ran a hand up her belly and tucked his hand inside her bra, cupping one of her breasts "—I never forgot."

She slid from his lap and his warm touch. "I don't want to do this on the floor with a pizza box as my pillow."

"We've done it in a lot of crazy places."

"Oh, I remember, Wells." Using his shoulder as a prop, she struggled to her feet and held out her hand. "But it's been over four years and I want to take my time with you."

And it could be another four years.

He grasped her hand and stood up beside

her. "Then I want to brush my teeth and wash this pizza from my hands."

"You first." She bumped his hip with hers.

As he ran the water in the bathroom, Savannah grabbed a candle from the living room, lit it and placed it on the nightstand in Connor's bedroom, then turned down the covers on his bed.

When he emerged from the bathroom, she was perched on the edge of it in the darkened room in her underwear.

His eyes burned with a heat as hot as that candle flame. "Nice—and I don't mean the candlelit room, although that's a nice touch, too."

She patted the bed. "Make yourself comfortable. I'm going to brush my teeth, too."

Connor strode to the bed, braced his hands on the mattress on either side of her and kissed her flat against the bed. "I don't mind pizza breath."

"Not fair." She pressed her hands against his chest and he relented.

As she got up from the bed, he smoothed a hand across her bottom. "Hurry back."

When she got to the bathroom, she washed her hands and brushed her teeth. She combed her fingers through her hair and whispered to her reflection, "Just this once."

She practically skipped back into the bedroom and stopped short when confronted with the image of Connor stretched out on his bed, in the buff, the candlelight flickering across his sculpted form.

"Ooh, you didn't even give me the chance to take your clothes off, piece by piece."

He sat up, folding his arms behind his head. "I can get dressed again if you want."

"Don't you dare." She rushed toward the bed and jumped on the edge on her knees. She then straddled him and rained kisses across his shoulders and chest.

Connor reached up and unhooked her bra. He caressed her breasts, running his thumbs across her peaked nipples. "Mmm, talk about perfection. Your body is as lithe and beautiful as ever."

She fell against him, and he rolled over, pinning her beneath him. He trailed his hands down her sides, hooking his fingers in the waistband of her panties and sliding them off.

He left a path of scorching kisses from between her breasts to her stomach, twirling his tongue in her navel until she giggled.

She slapped his shoulder. "Don't make me laugh. This is serious business."

"I like to make you laugh, and you haven't done much of it in a while." He slid his hands beneath her derriere, and she raised her pelvis.

"You can make me laugh later. Right now, make me sigh, groan, moan."

He buried his head between her legs and made her do all those things and more. When her orgasm claimed her and she reached her peak, she even screamed out his name.

He kissed the echoes of that scream from her lips as his erection skimmed her belly.

She brushed her fingers along his tight flesh, and his frame shuddered. As he stretched out beside her on the bed, she continued to caress him and he took over the moaning and groaning and sighing.

He stifled a gasp and cinched her wrist with his fingers. "Ahh, I want to be inside you."

"I'm yours for the taking—always was, always will be."

He reached for the drawer on the nightstand and yanked it open. He withdrew a blue foil square and held it up between two fingers. "You wanna help me with this?"

She swallowed and pasted a smile on her face. They hadn't been together for years, but she'd been willing to make love to him without a condom. But he wasn't.

"Any excuse to touch you there." She snatched the condom from his fingers and ripped the foil open with her teeth.

Seconds later, Connor eased into her and she closed around him. She wound her legs around his torso as he drove into her over and over, and the only thing pounding into her brain along with the rhythm of his thrusts was *he doesn't trust you, he doesn't trust you.*

Panting, he balanced on his elbows above her and peppered her face with feverish kisses. "Are you going to come? I can wait."

She dribbled her fingertips across his flushed face, damp with sweat. "Go ahead. I already experienced my paradise."

He kissed her again and moments later his body stiffened before he plowed into her hard and fast, gasping out his release.

He lay motionless on top of her for a few seconds before rolling off her body. He stroked the side of her breast. "Was I smothering you?"

"Only in the best of ways." Her fingers traced the outline of the muscles on his flat stomach.

He removed the condom and put it on a tissue on the bedside table. Reclining on his back again, he took her hand and laced his fingers with hers. "Just like old times. Better."

"Except for the protection."

His fingers tightened on hers for a second. "It's been a while since we've been together, Savannah."

Her heart began pounding, and she placed a hand against her chest in a lame attempt to steady it. "I killed him."

Chapter Twelve

The warm glow encasing him turned to ice and he jerked, Savannah's words like a physical jolt to his body.

His fingers, still entwined with hers, froze. Blood pounded in his ears and his jaw locked.

"Did you hear me?" Her voice, soft as a whisper, tickled his ear.

It broke the spell and he snatched his hand away from hers and bolted upright, the sheen of sweat on his body from making love to Savannah now giving him a chill.

"I heard you." His own voice came out like gravel on the pavement. "You killed Niles."

Savannah shot up against the headboard. "God, no. I didn't kill Niles."

Connor jerked his head to the side. What kind of games was she playing? "What the hell are you talking about? You told me you killed him."

"Not Niles. I killed *Manny*. I killed my stepfather."

A second jolt zapped his body, but this one juiced him with adrenaline, and he scrambled from the bed. "What do you mean? My father killed Manny for your mother, and then you and Georgie lied for him, telling the cops it happened in a self-defense, life or death struggle between my father and Manny."

She raised those violet eyes to his, her fingers twisting into knots over her naked body. "No. It didn't happen that way, Connor."

He shook his head. "You lied to me. *He* lied to me. My father paid with his life for killing Manny."

"I know that." She dropped her head, and her dark hair fanned out over her breasts.

He grabbed his boxers from the floor and

stepped into them. "Tell me everything. I want the truth—if you're capable."

Her hair swung in front of her face as she flinched. "Of course. I wanted to for the longest time."

She slid from his bed and pulled on her underwear, her back toward him. Then she grabbed the T-shirt he'd been wearing that day from on top of his dresser and pulled it over her head. She sat on the edge of the bed, stuffing her hands beneath her thighs.

"Not here." He jerked his thumb over his shoulder. "In the living room."

He turned his back on Savannah and the awful truths flowing from her lips. How could she be responsible for Manny's death? Why? Had she been trying to protect her mother, as Connor's father had claimed he'd been trying to do?

His anger and sense of betrayal fogged his brain, but he had to get past it long enough to listen to her, to find out what had really happened.

He collapsed on the couch amid the wreckage of their night and kicked the half-empty pizza box out of his way.

Savannah, twisting the hem of his shirt in her hands, followed him, and sank into the chair across from the couch. "I wanted to tell you so many times, Connor, but I didn't know how."

"You figured the best time was while I was providing an alibi for you for another murder and after we'd made love? That makes a lot of sense."

"The time seemed right—necessary."

He sliced a hand through the air. "Tell me how it happened."

"Manny had been harassing me." She licked her lips. "Coming on to me."

"Sexually?" He swallowed, the tightness in his throat almost unbearable.

"Yes."

"Since when? Not when he first married your mother? Not when you were fourteen?" His hands curled into fists on his knees. If Manny weren't already dead, he could kill him himself.

"No, at least he wasn't into young teens, but as soon as I turned eighteen he started making moves. It began the first time I came home from college, at Thanksgiving."

He remembered that time. He'd been so happy to have Savannah home, and any changes in her behavior he'd put down to college life.

"Did you tell Georgie?"

"Of course I did, and I told Manny off in no uncertain terms."

"What was your mother's response?" Connor clenched his jaw. He knew Georgie and could figure out how she'd react to her husband of five years, a husband showering her with cars, gifts and money, showing interest in her beautiful eighteen-year-old daughter.

Savannah twisted her lips. "Mom didn't like it and she even talked to Manny, but she told me to grow up and handle it. There was no way she was kicking Manny out."

"Didn't think so." Connor raised his eyes to the ceiling. "This started when you were eighteen and went on for three years before…before you killed him?"

"His interest in me would wax and wane. Sometimes he'd come on hard, putting his hands on my body, trying to kiss me, and other times he hardly noticed my presence."

Connor's stomach churned. "And Georgie was okay with all of this?"

"She wasn't okay with it, Connor, but she didn't want to make waves. She had a good setup with Manny."

"You didn't."

"No." She ran her pinkie finger across her bottom lip.

"What happened? What changed the night he was killed?"

"I'm not completely sure."

"What?" He hunched forward, digging his elbows into his knees. "You don't remember something like that?"

She finally raised her gaze to his and held it for a few beats. "I blacked out that night."

Connor fell back against the couch cushions, smacking the heel of his hand against his forehead. "Are you kidding me?"

"Would I kid about something like that? I can't remember what happened." Her knees started bouncing and she clamped her hands on them. "Mom told me Manny tried to rape me. He'd ripped off my clothes and cornered me in my room. I must've escaped, grabbed his gun where he kept it by the front door and shot him."

Connor dug his fingernails into his scalp, sympathy for Savannah and what she'd had to endure making inroads into his shock. "Where was Georgie when all this was going on? Why wasn't she there to protect you?"

"She had gone to a friend's house, but her friend wasn't feeling well so she turned around and came back." Savannah rolled her shoulders forward and hugged herself around the baggy T-shirt. "Mom said she came home, found me naked with a wide-eyed blank stare, crouching in the corner of the living room, with Manny's dead body across from me and the gun on the floor."

"Then she called my father."

"Of course. Who else?"

Just as Savannah had come running to Connor when she'd found herself with another dead body.

He took a deep breath. "And the two of them concocted the story of Manny physically attacking Georgie, who then called my father. And when he arrived, Manny pulled his gun on him, the two wrestled for control and the gun went off, killing Manny."

"Yes."

"Why didn't my father just leave it at that? Why did he tell my mother that he'd killed Manny outright instead of giving her the made-up story about Manny pointing the gun at him? Why heap further blame on himself?"

Savannah pressed her hands to her cheeks. "That was my mom's idea. She thought she'd come out looking better and it would keep your mother from talking if the chief owed something to Mom. I know. It's twisted."

"And your mother did all this to protect you? A little late. I can't imagine what you went through." He raised his hand and dropped it.

She noticed the gesture and swallowed. "Because I blacked out and I didn't have any injuries, she thought the police might not believe it was self-defense on my part. Hell, I don't even know if it was."

"Except for the fact that you had no clothes on and were in shock." Connor pounded a fist into the cushion next to him. "Why didn't you tell me? Why didn't my father?"

"It was all so messed up. Then your father lost his life because of me and my mother. If we'd told the truth, Manny's associates would've had no reason to go after your dad."

"Maybe they would've gone after you instead."

Her eyes widened. "A twenty-one-year-old college student who was warding off a rape? I don't think so."

Connor tilted his head back, resting it against the cushion, and stared at the ceiling. "Savannah, don't you think it's strange that you blacked out twice and both of those times you come to with a dead body?"

"Of course."

"And it never occurred to you that the same thing that happened with Manny happened with Niles?"

"Did I imply it never occurred to me? It did, but that's why I checked everything at the house. There was no evidence I stabbed Niles—no cuts on my dominant hand, no blood on my clothes or body, no sign that I showered off any blood. Nothing. I didn't do it, Connor. The police haven't found any evidence of my guilt."

He squeezed his eyes closed and pinched the bridge of his nose. "When did you regain consciousness, or whatever, the night Manny died? And what's the last thing you remember about that night?"

"I remember being home earlier and Mom going to her friend's." Savannah twisted a lock of hair around her finger. "I wasn't too worried about being home alone with Manny because he'd been preoccupied all summer, barely giving me a glance, which was a huge relief. Still, I remember changing into my pajamas, locking my bedroom door and watching some TV. That's it. I don't remember leaving the room. I don't remember Manny coming into the room. I sure as hell don't remember taking a gun and shooting at him."

He scratched his chin. "Where were you when you woke up, or came to? I don't even know what to call it."

"I was sitting on our couch, in my pajamas. Manny was dead on the floor and your dad and my mom were crouched over him." She trapped her hands between her knees. "I panicked. I screamed. I cried. I didn't know what was going on."

"Your mother told you what had happened?"

"She came to me and grabbed my hands. She told me she'd discovered me naked in the corner when she got home, Manny dead. I was numb, unresponsive, but she figured out what had happened. She dressed me and called your father, and they were going to fix everything between the two of them. She had me wash my hands—to get rid of the gun residue—and then she told me the story they were going with. That Manny had got abusive, belligerent, so she called Chief Wells, who was off duty. The chief arrived, Manny had a gun on us and then turned it on your father. He lunged for it, they struggled and the gun went off, killing Manny."

"I wish…" Connor grabbed a pillow and chucked it across the room. "I wish you'd told me—all of it. I wish you'd told me Manny was bothering you. Why didn't you?"

"I don't know." She lifted her shoulders. "I felt ashamed, like somehow I'd invited his attentions. Th-that's what my mom implied."

Heat thumped through his body and a pure hatred for Savannah's selfish, vain mother beat at his chest. How could his father have worshiped that woman? "That's ridiculous."

"I didn't want to tell you, Connor. You saw me through some kind of rose-colored glasses. I never knew why, but I didn't want that to end—ever. That's why I never told you any of it."

"Your secrecy destroyed our relationship anyway." He clasped his hands behind his neck. "That's why, isn't it? That's why you ran, that's why you married Niles."

"I killed someone and then put the blame on your father, who ended up paying for it with his life." She sniffled and rubbed her nose. "I didn't think that was something you could ever get past... Could you? Can you?"

Folding his body in half, Connor leaned forward, almost touching his head to his knees. "I don't know, Savannah. I can't believe you've lived with this burden these past years. When you woke up with Niles, you must've relived everything."

"I'm sorry, Connor. For everything. I never should've come here. I'm just like my mother and I tried so hard not to be her."

His head shot up. "You're nothing like Georgie."

Several seconds of heavy silence hung between them.

"What now?" She folded her hands in her lap, her knuckles white.

"We carry on as before. We get to the bottom of what happened the night Niles died…and that's going to start when you see Thomas tomorrow. No holding back." He leveled a finger at her. "Promise."

"I promise. I'll tell Thomas everything." She rose to her feet in a jerky movement and stooped to pick up the pizza box on the floor.

"Leave it. Go back to bed. You have a busy day tomorrow."

She hesitated, dropped the box and took a step back. She threw him a glance from beneath her lashes.

Folding his arms, he closed his eyes. "Go to bed, Savannah."

"Yours?"

"I'll be in later."

She shuffled down the hallway, his T-shirt floating around her body.

His muscles coiled as he fought the urge to go after her, take her in his arms, comfort her for what she'd endured as a frightened young woman. Then he sank back against the couch, placing his fingertips against the throbbing drumbeat in his temples.

If Savannah had blacked out and killed once, she could've blacked out and killed again.

Chapter Thirteen

The following morning, Savannah rolled over and buried her face in the pillow, the scent of Connor engulfing her and permeating all her senses. Connor, the man she'd loved…and betrayed.

The look in his blue eyes last night had told her everything she needed to know—justified her silence all those years. He hated her. Didn't trust her.

And she didn't blame him.

She ran her hands over the covers, which she'd straightened out last night, and knew Connor hadn't been back to bed—at least not this one.

A tap at the door had her sitting up and clutching the sheets to her chest. "Yes?"

"I have some breakfast for you, if you're interested."

She stared at the door handle, but Connor wasn't coming in. His footsteps faded down the hallway.

She scooted out of the bed and shed his T-shirt. Before she bunched it up and put it back where she'd found it, she hugged it against her stomach. She'd lost him.

She took a quick shower and pulled a pair of shorts and a blouse from her bag, then dressed in record speed. She scooped her hair into a ponytail, took a deep breath and went to meet her accuser.

As she turned the corner toward the kitchen, he held up a plate. "Eggs and toast okay again? I can get some grocery shopping done while you're seeing Thomas."

On her way into the room, she stubbed her toe on the smooth wood floor. Had Connor had his own blackout and forgotten what she'd told him last night?

He placed the plate of food on the counter and turned away. "I already ate. I'm going to shower before A.J. gets here. He's gonna pick up the knife and the scotch. It's time we got some answers—finally."

He hadn't forgotten a thing.

He exited the kitchen and called over his shoulder, "The security company is coming this morning, too."

Even though he'd already discussed setting up a security system at the house, his words carried an ominous tone—like he was warning her not to try anything.

She stabbed a clump of scrambled egg. Now she was just getting paranoid.

She held her fork suspended over her plate as she listened to the water run in the shower. If she could've kept her mouth shut last night, she might be enjoying that shower with Connor right now. Nothing had changed between them physically. The passion burned between them hotter than ever. Their bodies fitted together seamlessly. She hadn't been able to tell where hers ended and his began. But after he'd pulled out the condoms, it had all seemed like a lie. Hot sex was one thing, but true love required trust.

Someone knocked on the front door and Savannah dropped her fork. She spun around on the stool and hopped off. When she reached the door, she peered through the peephole at a buff guy with a shaved head, a gym bag over his shoulder.

Resting her hands against the door, she asked, "Who is it?"

"Ah, A.J. I'm here to see Connor Wells."

She cranked the dead bolt to the right and opened the door. "Hi, I'm Savannah."

A.J. inclined his head. "Hi, Savannah. Wasn't expecting anyone out here with Connor."

"C'mon in." Connor hadn't revealed all her dirty little secrets to A.J.? What did he think he was doing here?

Connor swooped into the living room, hand outstretched. "Hey, bro. Thanks for coming. You met Savannah?"

"I did." A.J.'s eyes narrowed. "Savannah Wedgewood, right?"

"I prefer Martell, but yeah, that's me. The merry widow." Savannah clenched her teeth behind her smile.

A splash of red stained A.J.'s bald pate. "Sorry. I just put two and two together."

"You still in?" Connor cocked his head at his friend.

"Are you kidding? Of course. Maybe I can crack the biggest murder case of the year." A.J. rubbed his hands together. "Give me the details."

"We're not giving you any details, A.J. Not yet anyway." Connor strode across the room to the fireplace and unzipped the black canvas bag. He dipped his hand inside and pulled out the crystal decanter. "We need this analyzed for any added substances, drugs."

A.J. took the decanter and swirled it so that the liquid sloshed up the sides. "Easy enough."

"And then there's this." Connor spread open the plastic bag and held it in front of him.

Even though A.J. must've known what to expect, his eyes widened. "This will be harder, but I think I can get a guy. Whose blood am I looking for?"

"Wait." Savannah held up her hand and pounced on her purse. She plunged her hand inside and pulled out a stiff piece of carpet. She cupped it in her palm and held it out to A.J. "This is Niles Wedgewood's blood."

Connor hunched over her hand and poked at the material with his fingertip. "Where did you get this?"

"From the house yesterday afternoon. It's part of the carpet that was underneath Niles's body."

"You cut off a piece? When?" Connor drew back, his eyebrows slamming over his nose.

"Of course not," she snapped. "The rug must've been sliced during the attack and this piece was hanging by a thread. I ripped it off. It's a lot better than A.J.'s friend raising red flags by trying to get the report on Niles's blood, isn't it?"

"It sure is." A.J. dipped his hand in the gym bag still hitched over his shoulder and shook out a plastic bag. "Drop it in here. Anything else?"

Savannah pinched the rug between two fingers and slipped it in. She rubbed her fingers together even though the blood on the rug was dried up. "You'll need to test it for my blood, too."

A.J. dropped the plastic bag and stooped over to retrieve it. When he straightened up, a light sheen of sweat had broken out across his forehead. "Is there something I should know?"

"Nothing." Savannah tossed back her hair. "It's just for ruling-out purposes, because *some people* need more proof than just someone's word."

Connor crossed his arms and clenched his jaw.

"All you have to do is poke your finger

and squeeze out a few drops onto a card or something."

"I can do that." She rested a finger on her chin. "Or maybe Connor wants to do the honors. He'd like to make me bleed right now."

Connor threw up his hands. "Do not ascribe acts of violence to me. I do not want to see you bleed."

A.J. cranked his head back and forth between the two of them. "If you wanna give me your blood, Savannah, I'll get out of here."

"You're scaring him off." Connor marched to the kitchen and yanked open a drawer. "Here's a safety pin. I'll hold it under a flame for a few seconds to sterilize it and then you can poke the hell out of yourself."

Savannah put a hand on her hip. "Told you."

Connor snorted, cranked on the flame beneath a burner and held the tip of the safety pin in the fire with a set of tongs. Then he swiped a piece of paper towel across the tip. "Don't want that black carbon in your skin."

As she took the pin from him, she skewered him with her gaze and tilted her head to the side. His joking manner indicated he'd loosened up a bit, but they still weren't back on solid ground. Would they ever be? Had they ever been since the night she'd shot Manny and blamed his father?

She pressed her thumb against the tip of her index finger and squeezed the skin tight. Then she jabbed her flesh with the tip of the pin. A bubble of blood formed immediately, so she held her finger over a note card and let the blood drip onto the surface.

She looked up at A.J. "Is that enough?"

"Plenty. You'd be surprised how little blood is needed for a good read these days."

A shiver ran up her spine as she plucked a wet paper towel from Connor and wrapped it around her finger. Had the crime scene investigators found a spot of her blood in Niles's bedroom?

A.J. waved the card in the air. "I'll just let

this dry for a few minutes before sealing it in a plastic bag, and then I'll be out of your hair."

"I really appreciate this, A.J." Connor clapped his friend on the shoulder. "Let us know the results as soon as you get them."

"Do you want anything to drink before you leave?" Savannah opened the fridge door to pull out the orange juice.

"No, thanks." He shook out another plastic baggie. "I'm waitin' on the wine to start flowing out of this place. How much longer, Connor?"

"I'll harvest the grapes from next year's crop, and that'll start the process."

"Good thing you're independently wealthy." A.J. slid a glance toward Savannah.

Connor did have money and property, but that look at her meant A.J. probably knew about her wealth, which was about to explode. Every article about Niles's death so far had mentioned her and what she stood to gain from the murder.

A.J. left, promising to get back to them as soon as he had the results.

Savannah glanced at her phone. "Just over an hour until I see Thomas. When is the security company getting here?"

"Should be here any minute." Connor jerked a finger toward his laptop. "I'm going to do some work, and then we can drive over together once the security company gets here—if that's still okay."

"It's still okay with me." She rinsed her glass out in the sink, her head hanging, her hair creating a curtain around her face. "I'm sorry, Connor."

"I know. I… I can't imagine what you've lived with these past years. You should've seen someone, a therapist like Thomas to help you cope."

Tears flooded her eyes and she swiped a hand across her stinging nose. "My mom told me not to go. She was afraid I could still get in trouble."

"Yeah, right." Connor huffed out a breath and strode toward his laptop.

While he met with the security company, Savannah spent the time on Snap App business and replying to emails. She sent one to Dee Dee, asking about archived files. She didn't know what the person who'd stolen that folder from her hoped to discover or hide. Niles had already reviewed that file. In fact, the folder was dog-eared. If it was something someone was trying to hide, it was too late for that.

Shortly after she sent an email to Nick Fresco, Snap App's CFO, he called her on her cell.

"Sorry I haven't called before now, Savannah. I didn't know what to say. The three of us were a team at the beginning…before the trouble between you two."

"I know, Nick. It's terrible. How's the vibe at the company?"

"Hard to judge. It's quiet here. You *did* tell people to take some time off, didn't you, boss?"

Savannah's gut tightened. Was that some

kind of dig at her? "You don't think that was a good idea?"

"Great idea. Looking forward to having you back here full-time, if…"

"If what?" Savannah gripped the phone. Nick always was the king of implication.

"Just wondering if those detectives are investigating you, Savannah. Do you think you need an attorney? I know Niles's guy, Neelon, isn't a criminal attorney, but he could recommend someone."

"Whoa, slow down. The cops aren't looking at me for this. I had an alibi that night. I wasn't even in San Diego at the time of the murder."

Nick clicked his tongue—another annoying habit he had. "I'm sorry. Didn't mean to hit a nerve there. I just thought…you know, the spouse is always the number one suspect, especially the ex-spouse."

"You should know, Nick. You have two of them."

"Okay, okay. Don't need to get snippy." He chuckled, which sounded totally fake to her.

"What about Brian Donahue?" She waved at Connor, who'd stepped through the front door and was jerking his finger over his shoulder.

Nick sucked in a breath. "What about Donahue?"

"You're the one who fired him. Do you think he did it?"

"No way. Going postal in an office shooting, maybe, but not a planned murder like this." He cleared his throat. "Do you need any help with the meeting tomorrow? I know you've been out of the loop for a while and Niles probably wasn't all that forthcoming with you."

"Thanks for the offer, but this is going to be more of a pep talk and a 'rah-rah, the fight will go on' kind of meeting."

"A few people are filtering back into the office today. Of course, they're upset about Niles, but they're also worried about their jobs."

"Their jobs aren't going anywhere. Despite some losses, the company's in good shape."

"Losses?"

"I need to talk to you about a few things, Nick. Can we have a meeting after the meeting?"

"Of course, but I don't know about any losses. Are you telling me Niles has been hiding a few facts and figures?"

"Not sure yet. We'll discuss." She waved at Connor, who was practically hopping from foot to foot by the door. "Have the homicide detectives interviewed you yet?"

"You mean good cop Krieger and bad cop Paulson?"

She slid from the kitchen stool and hung her purse over her shoulder, which sagged in relief. "Oh, you found them that way, too?"

"I guess it's standard procedure, but yeah. Paulson's the one who grilled me about my alibi and my position in the company. Real jerk."

Connor had walked outside, leaving the front door open, and Savannah scrambled to follow him out. Probably thought she was stalling.

"We'll talk more tomorrow, Nick. Thanks for phoning, and I'm sorry I snapped at you." She ended the call and got into the passenger seat beside Connor. "Nick Fresco, our... my CFO."

"Maybe he knows what's in that missing file, if it covered financials."

"We're having a meeting after my pep talk tomorrow." She put on her sunglasses and cracked the window. "Are you coming with me to the police station after my session with Thomas?"

"Do you want me to?"

"I do—even though you don't owe me anything now. Hell, you could turn me in if you wanted to."

He ran his hands up and down the steering wheel. "I never did any of this because I felt I owed you something, Savannah. You don't know that by now? You don't know how I feel about you? How I've always felt about you?"

She gave him a quick side glance from beneath her lashes. "How you used to feel about me before I spilled my guts and told you about Manny?"

He closed his eyes, and his nostrils flared. "I still love you, Savannah—no matter what you've done."

She let the words hang in the car, savoring their sweetness, ignoring the bitter undertone. He might love her and she sure as hell loved him, but that didn't mean they could ever overcome their baggage and be together. Heck, Connor still wasn't entirely convinced she didn't kill Niles, and maybe Letty, too, for that matter.

She folded her hands in her lap and stared out the window. "I know that."

Fifteen minutes later, Connor swung his truck into a small parking lot behind a two-story office building. He shifted into Park but didn't turn off the engine.

"Give Thomas my best. I'm heading over to the police station. They called me this morning while you were still asleep and told me they had some evidence against Jimmy Takata."

"Well, that's one mystery solved." She opened the car door and slid out. Then she ducked her head back inside and said, "I love you, too, Connor."

She slammed the door and hustled toward the stairs on the outside of the building, running away from Connor and her feelings for him.

When she got to Thomas's office, she tried the doorknob. It was unlocked and she pushed through. He had a small anteroom with a rack of magazines and four chairs, two on each side of a healthy potted plant. The sign next to a button on the door invited his clients to press it.

She did, listening for the echo of it in the office. Must've been hooked up to a light, because Thomas opened the door to his inner sanctum seconds later.

She held out her hand to the thinly built African American man with the warmest smile she'd ever seen. "I'm Savannah Martell."

"Welcome, Savannah. Thomas Bell." After

he shook her hand he waved his own toward his cozy office. "Have a seat anywhere."

Her gaze floated across the sofa and a deep leather armchair, a table with a box of tissues on it situated between the two. She opted for the other chair and sank into its embrace, already feeling at ease for some reason.

"Would you like some water, coffee, tea?" He cupped a mug of steaming brew in one hand.

"No, thanks."

Thomas settled into the chair across from hers and balanced his cup on his knee. His dark eyes met hers, one eyebrow slightly shifting, but otherwise he remained mute.

She tugged on a lock of her hair. "Umm, my ex-husband was murdered—and I blacked out. I was there, at the scene, but I swear I didn't kill him."

"You blacked out."

"Yes, but there was no evidence that I'd killed him. If there had been… I would've stayed and called the police."

"Do you typically have blackouts?"

"Only once before."

Thomas waited. He even took a sip of tea.

After a few stammering beginnings, Savannah poured out the entire story of Manny's death, her role in it, the cover-up.

She hadn't even finished the entire tale when Thomas glanced at his watch for the fifth time in five seconds. "We'll have to wrap it up here, Savannah."

She gawked at him, eyes wide, mouth open. "Is—is that it? What are you going to do?"

He steepled his fingertips. "Do you want me to do anything?"

She licked her lips. "I want to know what happened that night Manny was killed."

"You just told me what happened."

"I told you what I remembered and what my mother told me happened." She rubbed her upper lip. "I want to remember on my own, *my* memories."

"We can do that. Have you ever been hypnotized?"

"No, but I want to be if you think I can recover those memories."

"What about the other memories? The ones from a few nights ago—the other murder."

Savannah shot forward in her seat. "Those were different. I was drugged. I'm sure of that, and pretty soon I'm going to have the proof—to show Connor."

"It's important for you to show Connor."

"Of course."

Thomas hunched forward out of his seat. "Can you come back tomorrow for a hypnosis session?"

"Yes."

He slid his laptop from his desk and returned to his seat. "You can have my first appointment, at nine o'clock. Can you make that?"

"I'll be here." And she meant it. Now that she'd revealed the truth to Connor, she wanted to know the whole truth herself. She wanted to know if she was a cold-blooded killer or if Manny had given her no choice.

Could she have run from the house that

night? Fought him off? Called Connor? She'd chosen to shoot Manny through the heart instead and she wanted to know why.

When she reached the parking lot, she spotted Connor talking to a cop, both of them standing next to his truck.

She got a hitch in her step and swiped her damp palms on the back of her shorts, but she forced a smile and approached them. "Parking ticket?"

Connor turned toward her. "Good news."

Savannah eked out a sigh. "What?"

"Jimmy Takata just confessed to firebombing my shed. The police traced the jar used for the Molotov cocktail back to Jimmy's grandmother, and they even matched the print from his size nine flip-flops."

"Crack detective work." Savannah smiled at the cop.

"Hope to do the same for your ex-husband's murder case, ma'am."

Savannah's smile froze on her face. Was that a dig at her? A fishing expedition?

She rolled back her shoulders. "Thanks. I hope so, too."

When the fresh-faced cop left and they got into the truck, Connor turned toward her. "Everything okay?"

"Everything is fine. I'm going back tomorrow morning, first thing."

"Really?" He put the truck in gear and pulled out of the parking lot.

"Thomas is going to put me under. I'm going to try to find out what happened the night Manny died."

Connor paused and tensed his hands on the steering wheel. "And the night Niles died?"

She smacked her knee. "I'm telling you. That was different. I was drugged that night."

"I'm glad, and that's all I'm going to say." He brushed his knuckles against her thigh. "Do you want lunch before heading to San Diego and your interview with the detectives?"

"Of course." She squared her shoulders against the seat. "Fortification."

Over a lunch of fish tacos, their talk in the restaurant revolved around Jimmy Takata's arrest for setting the fire at Connor's place. A few side glances were thrown her way, but most of the people in San Juan didn't know Niles Wedgewood and didn't care about his death...even if they did know her connection to him.

Lunch ended all too soon and she and Connor hit the road to San Diego and her second interview with the police.

"Have you looked at the other files I took from Niles's desk or that flash drive?" he asked.

"No."

"I'm just wondering if the flash drive might contain the file that was stolen—you know, like a backup."

"Maybe." She drummed her fingers on the dash. "I didn't even check the file I took from Niles's desk."

"How do you know it was the one you wanted?"

"It was labeled. Niles was always very

careful about labeling and marking every-thing properly. Even his computer files are organized."

"Sounds like he'd be the type to back up stuff, even beyond the normal archiving. You should take a look."

"Will do." At least Connor had stopped growling at her and flaring his nostrils, but now they'd reached a level of civil, business-like discourse. Except for when he told her he loved her.

She pressed a hand against her belly. She'd keep those words safe and hold them close for when she was back on her own, back in San Diego running Snap App. She'd take them out and cup them in her hands now and then, just to remember what it felt like to be loved by a man like Connor Wells.

"We're here." He pulled around the back. "Do you want me to wait? Come with you?"

"That would probably look weird—like I need support or something." Her phone buzzed. "I hope that's not them canceling on me."

She pulled out the phone, swept her finger across the text message and gasped.

"What is it?" Connor leaned over, bumping her shoulder.

She held her phone higher so he could see the picture of her hunching over Letty's dead body.

Chapter Fourteen

"Damn." Connor smacked his fist against the center console. "Same sender as before? Unknown?"

"Yes." Savannah's hand trembled and she curled her fingers around the phone. "Can you read the words?"

"Words?" Connor squinted at the display, but it was too unsteady for him to make out the text.

"It says 'in case they ask you.'" She dropped the phone in her lap. "He knows I'm here, Connor. How?"

"You talked about this appointment before, when he was still listening to you."

Savannah dumped the contents of her

purse in her lap and scrabbled through the items, sending some to the floor of the truck.

"What are you doing?"

"Looking for another pen. What do you think?" She grabbed a perfectly innocent-looking ballpoint from Thomas's office and chucked it out the window.

Connor circled her wrist with his fingers. "Stop. When you still had the pen in my house, you talked to the police about coming in today."

"But now?" She crushed the empty purse against her chest. "Right now, while I'm about to go in for an interview… And what does it mean? How did he get that picture?"

"He may have set up a camera in the warehouse."

"What does he plan to do with this picture? The button? The knife? If he's trying to set me up, why doesn't he just do it already?" She let out a scream. "I'd rather have him turn over everything to the police so I can see his endgame, start defending myself."

Connor reached over and squeezed the

back of her neck. "If he wanted to turn you in to the police, he would've done it already."

"That must've been his intention when he made the anonymous call about the knife in my trunk—because you know he's responsible for that." She tipped her head back as Connor kneaded her tight neck. "What changed?"

"I don't know. The alibi I gave you? The fact that you cleaned up and got the hell out of Niles's house that morning without a backward glance? Maybe he expected you to fall apart."

"Then he's obviously someone who doesn't know me well." She yanked open her purse and started shoveling her belongings back inside. "He can keep sending pictures and stupid texts—and I'm going to keep doing what I'm doing."

Connor's hand slid down and rubbed a circle on her back. "You always do, Savannah. You're a survivor."

She leaned back and trapped his hand between her body and the car seat. "I learned from the best—my mother."

He rescued his hand and cranked on the ignition. He didn't like her comparing herself to Georgie. Savannah lacked the grasping desperation of her mother.

"Get in there and survive." He tapped the phone in his pocket. "Text me when you're done."

She dropped a key chain in the cup holder. "Do me a favor?"

He'd offered her an alibi. How could he possibly refuse her anything? "Sure."

"Go to the La Jolla house and snoop around a bit more. If anyone discovers you there, you can claim to be checking on the cleaning crew you set up for Melanie. That's a legitimate reason."

"I wasn't done looking around anyway. I'll check it out. And, Savannah?" He smoothed a hand against her tousled hair. "It's gonna be okay."

She leaned forward in a burst and planted a hard kiss on his mouth. "Damn right it is."

He watched her walk toward the doors of the sheriff's department through narrowed eyes. The last time he'd dropped her off, she told him she loved him. This time she'd kissed him. How could he still believe she was a killer?

Because she was—she'd killed Manny.

As CONNOR PULLED the truck into the driveway of Niles's house, the scene of the crime, he released a breath. Niles's sister had left, or at least had gone out. Had she stayed overnight in the house where her brother had been murdered?

He jingled the keys in his hand as he walked up to the front door. The crime scene tape had been removed, most likely courtesy of the cleanup crew.

When he stepped across the threshold into the large foyer, he held his breath. He didn't know what he expected, but he raised his nose in the air and sniffed, the smell of bleach making his eyes water.

He took the stairs two at a time and entered the master bedroom. The drapes billowed into the room from the open French doors. The cleaning crew must've left the windows open to air out the place—not that a burglar could make his way up to the house this way...or a killer.

The reports mentioned no signs of a break-in that night, so Niles must've let his killer in—or he was already here.

As he walked toward the balcony, Connor skimmed his fingertips along the bed, stripped of its covers. No blood stained the mattress, and he'd noticed before, on his first trip, that the walls were free of blood splatter.

The stabbing had been controlled. That could've happened if Niles had been killed in his sleep...or in a drugged state. The killer could've rolled him out of bed or carried him upstairs, placed him on the floor and proceeded to rip up his flesh with the blade of a knife.

Connor had been a cop, not a crime scene investigator or even a detective. If he could figure this out, Homicide must've already come to that conclusion. The number of stab wounds Niles had should've resulted in blood droplets all over this room.

If Niles had been drugged, why not Savannah, too? Someone could've spiked the scotch; they both conked out downstairs and were carried up here and undressed. The killer placed Savannah in the bed, slicing her hand—the wrong one—and dumped Niles on the floor and stabbed him to death, leaving Savannah to wake up with a dead body. Probably figured she'd panic, thinking she'd never get away with this, not remembering what happened, and that she'd call the police.

The killer obviously didn't know Savannah. Tiffany? That woman never could've pulled this off herself. Maybe Denny, with or without Tiffany's help.

Why set up Savannah? Connor twitched back the drapes and stepped onto the balcony, inhaling the salty sea breeze. The knife, the button, the incriminating picture with Letty—that could all be for blackmail purposes, especially once they realized Savannah had no intention of caving and copping to a murder she didn't commit—or at least one she couldn't remember committing.

She didn't remember killing Manny, either.

Bracing his hands on the stucco wall that separated him from the waves crashing on the rocks below, he leaned forward, feeling the breeze lift the ends of his hair from the back of his neck.

Why had his father continued to lie to him about that night? And to Mom? Hadn't he realized it had wrecked Connor's faith in him? Knocked him off that pedestal his son had been constructing since the time he was a small boy and dreamed of being just like his dad?

Georgie had done that to his family. Georgie had sacrificed her own daughter, as well. Sacrificed her to a low-life drug dealer in exchange for a fancy car, diamonds and trips to Vegas to fuel her gambling habit. She'd forced Savannah into the position she'd found herself in that night—facing a rapist in her own home.

Connor shook his head and pulled back from the drop-off. He turned to face the room and inspected every corner of it.

No more buttons. No more blood. No more evidence linking Savannah to the murder. The cleanup crew had done a bang-up job.

Connor closed his eyes, trying to imagine Savannah waking up in this room with her ex-husband dead on the floor. Most women would've panicked and run, without a thought to any evidence left behind, or maybe most women would've called 911. Savannah wasn't most women.

His eyelids flew open as a frisson of fear tickled the back of his neck. Murder changed a room—a house. All the bleach in the world couldn't erase the bad vibes that hung over this space like a dark curtain.

As Connor walked out of the room, he said aloud to no one, "Poor sap."

Had Niles's fate been sealed the day he fell in love with Savannah? Had his?

Connor jogged down the stairs and crossed the great room to the office. He searched through Niles's desk again, rapping his knuckles against the space on the desk where a computer should be. Too bad they couldn't get their hands on that computer.

The cyberforensics team at the sheriff's department would give it the once-over, but Savannah would be the one to know if the computer held any clues to Niles's murder.

Crouching, Connor pulled open the desk drawer with the false bottom. Maybe that missing file held the key to everything.

A slight whisper behind him made the hair on the back of his neck quiver. But before he could turn around something landed on the back of his head with a thump that echoed through his brain, and he slumped forward.

As his eyes drifted closed, he thought about Savannah blacked out in this house… and then everything went dark.

Chapter Fifteen

Savannah ordered a car from the ride app and then cupped her phone in her hand to track the driver's progress.

She planned to replace her phone as soon as possible now that she had proved to the police that the thing was on the fritz. They'd had plenty of questions about why she didn't have her phone the night of Niles's murder. The device had performed like a champ in the interview room with the detectives, losing 50 percent of its charge in the hour she'd been in there.

They hadn't asked her anything about Letty. She hunched her shoulders against the chill wending its way up her spine, which even the warm San Diego sun couldn't melt away. She hated the thought of Letty's body in that warehouse. Had her family reported her missing yet? Had anyone made the connection between Letty and Niles? Maybe the cops knew and were waiting for some kind of slipup on her part. Paulson was a sneaky bastard.

She tapped the toe of her sandal. Where had Connor gone? She'd texted him twice and called him. If he'd gone to the beach at the foot of the house, he may have lost service, but why would he be down there?

Maybe he'd had enough of her and had taken off to go home. Telling him about Manny had been one of the hardest things she'd ever done in her life—but necessary. Maybe the truth never could repair what was broken between them, but the lies never gave them a chance.

And she wanted a chance with Connor. Being with him the past few days had made it clear to her that she belonged with that man and no other.

If she stuck out this therapy with Thomas, maybe she and Connor could start fresh. Of course, she'd have to get past her current dilemma.

Damn Niles for getting himself killed. Nobody deserved murder, but Niles had been playing with fire for too long, juggling women and their exes.

Her ride pulled up to the curb in front of the sheriff's department and she hopped in. Even though she'd indicated the La Jolla address when she ordered the car, she still gave the driver directions, impatient to get to the house and find out where Connor went.

When the driver dropped her off, she blew out a sigh, seeing Connor's white truck parked out front.

She went up to the door and, rattling the handle, discovered it was locked. She banged on the solid wood. "Connor, are you in there?"

Stepping back, she tipped her head to scan the windows of the second story. He had her keys.

She went around to the side of the house and tried the sliding door to the kitchen. No luck. She pressed her nose against the glass and peered inside. The gleaming kitchen stretched before her—empty. Not that she expected Connor to be in there eating a sandwich.

Her steps a little quicker, her knees a little shakier, she went back to the front of the house and clambered through the flower bed outside Niles's office. Cupping her hands around her face, she looked through the window.

She let out a scream when she saw Connor crumpled on the floor behind Niles's desk. Dear God, not again.

She beat her fists against the glass. "Connor! Connor!"

Spinning around in the dirt, she scanned the ground and picked up a sizable rock. It was her house now and she didn't give a damn.

She smashed the rock against the windowpane closest to the handle. It took her three tries to break the glass.

When the window sported a jagged hole, she reached through and flipped up the lock, swung it open and stepped through, into the room.

Connor's body lay less than two feet away, and Savannah dropped to her knees beside him.

She placed two fingers against his neck and let out a sob when his pulse beat strong against her fingertips. She ran her hands over his face and chest. No blood.

Then she readjusted his head, and her hand came away wet and sticky. She gasped at the red stain on her palm.

"Connor, Connor."

She staggered to her feet and rushed to the wet bar. She grabbed a towel from beneath the sink and soaked it with water.

When she returned to Connor, she swiped the wet cloth across his face. "Connor, wake up. You're not dead."

She cradled his head in her lap and pressed

the damp towel against the wound on the back of his skull to staunch the flow of blood. Head wounds always looked worse than they were; Connor had taught her that.

"Connor, don't you dare leave me in this house with another dead body. Wake up, damn it." She patted his face—maybe a little harder than she intended.

His lips parted and he emitted some sound—not quite a word, but she'd take it.

"Connor!" She brushed her hand across his brow and tucked his hair behind his ear. "C'mon, baby. Come back to me. I need you."

His thick, stubby lashes fluttered and he muttered another incompressible word.

She slid his head from her lap and wedged the towel beneath his cut. She rose to her feet and returned to the wet bar, this time filling a glass with water. Her hand hovered over a decanter of whiskey. Maybe he needed something stronger. She poured the amber liquid into a second glass and returned to the patient carrying both drinks.

She sat cross-legged on the floor beside him and carefully lifted his head again. She put the glass of booze to his slightly parted lips and tipped a small amount of the liquid into his mouth.

Most of it ran down his jaw and neck, but he sputtered and blinked.

"Keep it going, baby. You can have the rest when you come to."

Connor groaned and her heart sang. He wasn't going to die on her.

He reached for his head and she swatted his hand away.

"You have a big gash on the back of your skull. I have that covered—literally." She curled an arm around his shoulders. "Does anything else hurt? I didn't see any other injuries. What happened, Connor?"

He struggled to sit upright, and she placed a hand on his shoulder. "Are you sure you should be moving around?"

He cleared his throat and winced. "I'm fine."

"Obviously not." She helped him sit up and

lean against the desk. "You were out cold when I got here, and must've been in that condition for quite some time because I've been trying to reach you to pick me up from the sheriff's department and you didn't answer."

His limbs jerked and his eyelids flew open. "How do you know it's safe? Someone hit me."

"Whoever attacked you is gone now. The house was locked up when I got here." She stirred the broken glass on the floor with her toe. "I had to break a window to bust my way in here."

His lip twitched. "Bust your way in?"

"Oh, you think that's an exaggeration?" She raised one eyebrow. "I peered in and saw you on the floor. I thought I had my third dead body on my hands in the space of a week."

He coughed. "Not dead."

"Here." She thrust the whiskey at him. "Down some of this. You still look a little white around the lips."

"Damn. He took me by surprise." He wrapped his long fingers around the glass and took a gulp.

"You didn't see him, I suppose."

"No."

"What were you doing? What does he want?" Savannah peeled the towel from Connor's head and parted his hair to inspect the small wound, which was still producing a steady stream of blood. She clamped the towel back on.

"This." Connor hit the desk drawer with his fist. "I was checking out Niles's secret hiding place again. That's when he hit me."

"How did he even get in? The house was locked up when I arrived." She tipped her head toward the gaping hole in the window. "You saw what I had to resort to."

"I have no clue, but I'm guessing he was here before I was. Hiding, maybe just like the night of Niles's murder. I didn't hear any noises in the house when I was upstairs, but I've been pretty clueless in general, allowing him to get the jump on me."

Savannah rolled her eyes. "Would you stop focusing on that? Why would he want any more of Niles's files? He stole the one he wanted from me, didn't he?"

"I don't know, but somebody wants these files and it seems as if it's someone who has access to the house." Connor switched the whiskey for the water and drained the glass. "Do you think Tiffany has keys to this house?"

"I'm sure of it. You think Tiffany whacked you on the back of the head hard enough to knock you out?"

"No, but her biker boyfriend could've done it."

"What do you think they want with information about the company?"

"Who says it's info about the company? It could be anything."

"You're right." She took his free hand and held it against the towel. "Hold this in place while I get another. I think it's finally stopped bleeding. Does it hurt?"

"Throbs."

She jumped up and got another towel, a dry one this time. "I have some ibuprofen in my purse."

When she returned to him, he struggled to his feet and she grabbed his arm. "You gave me a scare, Connor."

"Thanks for rescuing me. Who knows how long I would've been bleeding out on the floor?" He took the dry towel from her and folded it up against his head. "How'd it go with the detectives?"

"I think it went okay. They did have questions about my phone, but I was able to show them that it was broken. They didn't mention Letty at all, which is strange. Hasn't her family reported her missing?"

"Maybe they have and the sheriff's department hasn't made the connection yet." Connor sucked in a breath as he twisted his head from side to side. "Did you get your digs in about Tiffany and Denny? Tell them about Brian Donahue?"

"I told them I thought Denny was staying with Tiffany, and they already knew about

Brian. People at the office told them...and he's missing."

"Donahue is missing?"

Savannah dug into her purse and took out a little bottle of ibuprofen, shaking it in the air. "Maybe *missing* is too strong a word, but they haven't spoken to him yet because his mother said he went on a trip."

"He lives with his mother?"

"He does." She tapped out two gel caps and handed them to Connor.

"Did he take the trip before or after the murder?"

"They didn't tell me those details."

"Maybe Donahue's busy skulking around setting you up—two birds with one stone." Connor popped the pills into his mouth and washed them down with a shot of whiskey.

"That's what it feels like to me. Someone killed Niles, getting their revenge on him, and someone's setting me up and torturing me, getting their revenge on me. Two birds."

"You'd better make a call and get that window fixed while we're still here. You don't want anyone else breaking in. Might not be a bad idea to repair the security system when you get a chance." He crumpled up both towels, wrapping the wet one in the dry one. "Do you want these?"

"I think you should keep one in case your head starts bleeding again on the ride back to your place." She took out her almost-dead phone to find a glass repair place.

"Good idea." He shook out the towels and glanced at the wet one. "Do you want it?"

"Toss it in the trash." She held up her cell. "I just found a place with twenty-four-hour emergency repair."

"What are you going to do with this house, Savannah?"

"Sell it—at a reduced price."

"You'll always have to disclose the murder."

"Just like we did when we sold Mom's place."

Savannah placed a call to the glass repair company and explained the break. When she hung up, she said, "Can you stand to be here another hour or so? They can get here in twenty minutes."

"Sure, but when we get back, I want you to start looking at the files you do have. It's a good thing you locked them up." Connor took the two glasses to the bar and washed them out. "You can ask Dee Dee about the other one tomorrow."

"I plan to. I'm getting together with her before the general meeting and Nick after."

"When are you seeing Thomas? Didn't you say the two of you had another session to-morrow?"

"First thing in the morning." She pointed to the office door. "Let's wait somewhere else—outside preferably. I've had enough of this place."

THEY ROLLED INTO San Juan Beach around dinnertime. Even though Connor's new security system was programmed to notify his cell phone of any activity, he went straight to his laptop and looked at the footage.

He glanced up from clicking. "Just the mail carrier so far."

"That's good. Doesn't mean someone's not watching us." Savannah broke off a piece of banana and stuffed it in her mouth. "I feel like someone is tracking my every move—and yours. How did someone know you'd be at the house?"

"That was the pen. That's how he knew about Letty—or he set up Letty himself and that's how he knew you were heading to the interview with the detectives." He snapped his laptop closed. "It's also how he knew about the desk drawer. We were talking about it right before I discovered the pen wasn't a pen. And this time? Maybe he's just watching the house. Speaking of the desk drawers, are you going to pull out those files now?"

"I can't." She waved the banana at him. "They're in your safe and you didn't give me the combination."

"Don't take offense. I don't give anyone that combination."

"None taken." She snapped her fingers

twice. "But can you open it for me now? Nothing from A.J. yet?"

"Nope. You'll be the first to know." He disappeared into his bedroom, and she could hear him opening the closet door. He emerged moments later, clutching the files in one hand and dangling the flash drive from the fingers of his other. "Let's not forget this."

"Okay, I'm ready." She hopped onto a kitchen stool and patted the counter. "Let's see what Niles held near and dear."

"Not you, that's for sure."

When Connor dropped the file folders on the counter, Savannah grabbed his wrist. "I should've never married him."

"I could've told you that." He slipped from her grasp. "While you look at those, I'm going to do some work, and then we'll have dinner. Sound like a plan?"

"It does." She glanced at her charging phone. "As long as I don't get any more anonymous messages. I'm just waiting for the other shoe to drop. When is he going to turn that stuff he has on me over to the detectives?"

"He's not. He would've made a move by now. He wants something else."

"If it's not money, I don't know what he wants from me. Why doesn't he just ask?"

"He's trying to keep you unsettled."

"It's working."

"I'll pour you a glass of wine. You need it." Connor opened a cupboard and took down two wineglasses.

She flipped open the first folder and ran her finger across the text. It contained information about offers for the company—they'd had several. She sucked in her bottom lip and closed the folder, smoothing her fingertips over the edge of the label in the upper-right corner.

"What's wrong?" Connor set the glass of wine in front of her.

"This label does not match the contents of this file. All the paperwork in here deals with offers we received from other entities to buy out Snap App, and the label is for human resources."

"Misfiled?" Connor cupped his wineglass in both hands and swirled the ruby liquid.

"Niles didn't misfile anything—he was organized to a fault."

"You think he mislabeled the folders on purpose?"

"Maybe." She sat up straight. "So perhaps the file I took from the drawer the night Niles was killed, expecting financials from last year, didn't contain financials at all."

Connor stabbed a finger at the stack of folders. "And that's why someone cracked me on the head today in Niles's office. He stole the file from you yesterday and it didn't contain what he expected."

Savannah's pulse picked up speed. "The HR papers that should be in this folder might be in another one. There could be something in Brian Donahue's personnel record he doesn't want anyone to see."

"We're back to Brian?"

"Those detectives are sure interested in

him, since he's disappeared." Savannah shuffled through the remaining four folders, flipping through the papers inside. "No HR stuff at all, so the labels are totally random."

Connor touched his glass to hers. "I'll let you figure it out. Dinner in an hour?"

"Gotcha." She went back to the first folder and started skimming the offers. None surprised her, but she could understand why Niles would want to keep this information confidential.

She moved on to the next folder and flipped through some data on acquisitions—again, nothing earth-shattering, but nothing you wanted in a public forum or even employees to know about.

When she studied the spreadsheets in the next folder, her heart skipped a beat. "Here's the stuff I wanted in the first place, the stuff our thief thought he was stealing."

"Good. I guess Niles outwitted him."

Savannah trailed her finger down a column of numbers. "This is exactly what I was looking for. Payments received for orders placed for the past two years for our service contracts."

Connor called across the room, "That reminds me. I need to get a new accountant for the winery. Mine retired and I'm not great with numbers."

"You're not the only one." Savannah lodged the tip of her tongue in the corner of her mouth as she grabbed her charging phone and brought up the calculator.

As Savannah got deeper and deeper into the figures, her fingers became unsteady as she tapped in the numbers. Finally, she slumped forward and dropped her phone.

Connor looked up. "Get what you wanted?"

"Yes and no. It looks like Snap App's books have been cooked. Payments for deals we made for service contracts lasting several months have been reported in lump sums for the year. It's called accelerating the revenues."

"Explain to the dummy, please."

"So a company places an order with us for four million dollars for a four-year contract, with an agreement to pay us a million a year."

"Sounds sweet."

"Yeah, but these figures show we weren't amortizing the payments over four years, but reporting them as a lump sum in the year the contract was signed." She scooped up the papers and waved them in the air. "It's been done with several contracts, amounting to recorded payments in the hundreds of millions—payments that aren't real."

Connor shoved his computer from his lap and jumped up. "That's it, Savannah. Whoever falsified that information is the one who killed Niles and doesn't want you to discover his misdeeds."

"I know. There's just one problem with that deduction."

"What?"

"It was Niles who did it."

Chapter Sixteen

Connor hit the side of his head with the heel of his hand, as if to knock out his confusion. "I thought I had a handle on this."

"You do. Your theory would make total sense, but the truth is here in black and white. Niles has been fudging these numbers for two years." She tapped the folder. "He'd been keeping the real numbers along with the fake numbers so he wouldn't get confused, but the fake numbers are in the computer system. The fake numbers are the ones our stockholders are seeing—the ones I saw."

Connor circled the counter and faced Savannah. "His death is related to this. It has to be, but how? If someone found out and threatened to blackmail Niles, that person wouldn't kill him."

"Unless he confronted Niles, they got into a fight and the blackmailer stabbed Niles to death."

"That doesn't make much sense. When he killed Niles, he killed any chance for a payout." Connor turned the folder around to face him. "Savannah, Niles had no intention of giving you these spreadsheets. He knew you'd take one look at them and figure out his scam—just like you did."

"What are you saying?" She grabbed her wineglass and took a swig.

"Why did he invite you back to his house if he knew he wasn't going to give you the figures you were asking for?"

"Stall tactic?" She shrugged, but her violet eyes had turned dark.

"When you went back to his place, he gave you that scotch, didn't he? You saw your lipstick on the glass, so you know you at least took a few sips."

"Yes." Her fingers curled around the stem of her wineglass. "You're saying Niles is the one who drugged me?"

"Who else? It was his house, his scotch, his misdeeds."

"No, no." She slid from the stool and paced to the window. "You think Niles was going to kill me?"

Connor slammed his fist on top of the folder. "He wasn't going to give up those numbers. He wasn't going to tell you he'd been cheating and lying. He knew you'd never go along with that…didn't he?"

"Of course he knew that." Her eyes flashed at him.

"Sorry." He held up his hand. "Then the only reason for him to invite you back to the house and drug you was to kill you. Keep you from ever finding out what he'd been doing."

She closed her eyes and her chest heaved. "Even if I believe that—and I'm not saying I do—what went wrong? How did he wind up dead and I wind up scrambling to avoid an arrest for his murder?"

Connor's shoulders slumped. "That I don't know. Why was Brian Donahue fired?"

"Poor social skills. He couldn't get along with anyone he worked with and actually threatened our CFO. We had him escorted off the property." Savannah wrinkled her nose. "The whole thing was uncomfortable."

"Could he have been involved with this? It's obvious someone else knew what Niles was doing, or found out."

"But why wouldn't that person want it to come to light? Because that's why he's after this folder. He thought he stole this info from me the first time, and then thought he could get it from Niles's office when he bashed you on the head." She touched the back of her own head. "How's your wound anyway?"

Connor's eyebrows shot up. "That's hardly important right now…and it's fine. Maybe he's working so hard to get Niles's secret folders because there's some evidence of his blackmail scheme and even his murder of Niles."

Savannah slid the incriminating file away and pulled another one in front of her with a finger. "Last one to go through."

She flipped it open and squinted at the single page inside. "Oh, God."

"What now?" Connor leaned over her shoulder, taking in a bunch of names and dollar amounts. "What's this?"

"Niles's private payouts. Apparently, he was using the company funds for personal payments."

"What a piece of work. I'm surprised the company didn't collapse under him." The names blurred under his gaze and he rubbed his eyes. "Anything big enough for a blackmail payment?"

"Could be, but it's the names that are giving me pause—and making me sick to my stomach." She placed a hand on her belly.

"Like who?"

She skimmed the tip of her finger down the page. "He has payments here to Tiffany, which doesn't surprise me, but Dee Dee is on here. I can't imagine what that's for, and I don't think I wanna know."

He snatched the paper from her and flapped it in the air. "Looks like a list of suspects to me. That meeting with Dee Dee is going to be more interesting than you originally thought. Now, can we take this to dinner with us and pore over it while we eat? I'm gonna drop dead of starvation."

THE FOLLOWING MORNING, Savannah woke up in the guest bedroom. Connor had come a long way since the moment she'd confessed to Manny's murder, but making love again didn't seem like the right move…for either of them.

She had her hypnotherapy session to get through with Thomas this morning before heading to the office, which she was now dreading.

Why had Niles made an undercover payment to Dee Dee? To his sister? Why was he using company funds? And had he really been plotting her murder?

Connor tapped on the door. "I made some breakfast."

"Thanks. How's your head this morning?"

He cracked the door and poked his head into the room. "Sore and I have a big lump—bigger than the one you had when you arrived on my doorstep."

She reached back and traced the bump on the back of her head, wondering if it had been delivered by the same person who'd attacked Connor. "That seems like a lifetime ago."

"I'm glad you turned to me." Connor's face reddened to the roots of his hair. "And I'm sorry."

"For what? You took me in, lied for me, are helping me find out what happened that night. You have nothing to be sorry for."

Connor walked into the room and sat on the edge of the bed. He took both her hands in his. "I'm sorry I had my suspicions about you and the night Niles died."

"Someone was trying to set me up. Why wouldn't you have your suspicions? The truly amazing takeaway is that despite your suspicions, you took me in." She raised his hands to her lips and kissed his knuckles.

"Don't you already know I'd see you through anything?"

"Even though I killed Manny and blamed your father?"

He disentangled his fingers from hers and smoothed the covers over her thigh. "You act like you did that on your own, like it was your idea. You were a young woman in shock." When Connor's phone buzzed, he held up his finger. "Hang on. A.J.?"

Savannah scooted forward in bed, clutching the sheets.

Connor nodded. "I see. Thanks, man. I appreciate it. I owe you a case of wine when the time comes."

He ended the call. "You were right. The scotch showed traces of Rohypnol. You were roofied—and maybe Niles was, too."

Savannah fell back against the headboard, her nose stinging. "I knew it."

"Savannah, maybe it's time we go to the police."

She threw off the covers. "Are you crazy? We lied. *You* lied. You interfered with a police investigation, obstructed justice or whatever. You're not going down for any of this, Connor. I'm not going to allow that."

"This information that A.J. has could go a long way toward clearing you."

"Those detectives may suspect all they want, but they still have no proof I was there that night. I'm not going to give it to them and neither are you." She pushed at his broad back. "Now, get out of here. I have to shower and dress for my big day."

An hour later, Connor dropped her off in front of Thomas's office and she made her way up the stairs, her stomach fluttering. She'd skipped breakfast this morning and she knew she'd made the right move, as she felt like throwing up.

She followed the same protocol as last time

and settled into the chair across from Thomas's. "Should I lie down on the couch instead?"

"Wherever you're comfortable, Savannah."

She'd be comfortable in Connor's arms right now, but this chair would have to suffice. "I'm comfortable and ready."

Thomas opened his hand to reveal a silver pen. "Just something to focus on while I put you under."

"No watch swinging back and forth on a chain?" She giggled and put her hand over her mouth.

He smiled his patient smile. "We can do that, if you like."

"If the pen works, I'll do the pen." She clasped her hands between her knees.

"It works better if you're relaxed." He nodded toward her knees. "Put your hands at your sides or in your lap. Relax your muscles. Lean back in the chair. You look ready to blast off."

"I am." She let out a jagged breath and fell back against the chair.

Thomas began at once, his soothing voice acting like a salve on her nerves. When he told her that her eyelids were getting heavy, she blinked slowly and had a hard time lifting them. Her breathing deepened and her head bobbed once, twice.

They were arguing again.

"Who?" Thomas's voice had somehow found its way into the house she'd shared with her mother and Manny—a big house, bigger than anything they'd lived in before.

"Mom and Manny."

Arguing, always arguing. Why wouldn't Mom leave him? He bothered her—always found some excuse to touch her or stroke her hair. She hated him.

She covered her ears. She should go out. Call Connor. But Connor was a grown-up now. He'd graduated from the police academy with top honors. He'd be a cop, like his father, and always be there for her.

She'd go out there and tell them to knock it off, but she didn't want to get in the middle of one of their fights. If only the fight were about her. If only Mom was warning Manny to stay away from her.

But they were fighting about money. Mom wanted more.

She sat up and yanked the earbuds from her ears. Something had changed. Mom was threatening Manny. Threatening him with exposure. Mom was accusing Manny of dealing drugs.

She shimmied off her bed and pressed her ear against the bedroom door. *Stop, Mom.* She jumped back from the door when she heard a loud thump.

If Manny had hit Mom, she'd have to do something. Call the police.

Then she heard an even more terrifying sound.

"What did you hear, Savannah?"

"It's a gunshot."

She flung open her door and rushed into the living room. She screamed.

"What do you see, Savannah."

"Manny is on the floor, bleeding. Mom is

standing there with a gun in her hand. I'm screaming. I can't stop screaming."

Was she really screaming?

Mom dropped the gun and shook her. Shook her into silence. She couldn't speak. Couldn't move. She felt frozen. Suspended in space and time.

Mom's voice came at her from a long way away, but she couldn't understand her. Couldn't respond.

Mom shook her again. Slapped her face. She didn't even care. She wanted to curl up in a ball. She slumped in her mother's arms.

Mom pushed her away and grabbed her camisole. Mom ripped her camisole from her body. She didn't care.

Mom tugged down her pajama bottoms and her underwear. She didn't care. She wanted to curl into a ball and go far away.

Mom's voice filtered into her brain. "It's okay, Savannah. You didn't mean to do it. Manny tried to rape you."

Did he?

Mom's hands, soothing and protective,

stroked her arms. "Sit in the corner. I'll fix everything."

She sank in the corner, naked, confused, shocked. Mom would fix everything.

She blinked and met Thomas's steady gaze. Then she covered her eyes with one hand. "I remember. My mom shot Manny and blamed me."

Chapter Seventeen

Connor watched Savannah walk down the stairs, and his lips curled up on one side despite everything they were dealing with right now. He couldn't help himself.

As she got closer, the smile faded from his face and his gut twisted into knots. She had a tissue clutched in her hand and kept dabbing at her eyes and her nose. Her rounded shoulders made her look about two inches shorter and her hair hung on either side of her face, practically hiding it as she kept her gaze pinned to the ground.

Connor jumped from the Lexus and jogged toward her. "Savannah? Babe? What's wrong? What happened in there?"

Lifting her head, she raised her eyes, flooded with a fresh set of tears to join the ones rolling down her cheeks. "I learned the truth."

He swallowed and gritted his teeth, bracing for the worst. What could be more terrible than killing a man in self-defense? He dug his shoes into the asphalt. Killing a man in cold blood.

"What is the truth?"

"My own mother killed Manny—and she set me up and made me believe I'd done it." She emitted an animallike wail and dropped into a crouch at his feet.

A white-hot rage engulfed him like a wave and he staggered back. His hands clenched into fists.

Moaning, Savannah doubled over, wrapping her arms around her waist.

Connor's breath came out in gusts, and then he knelt beside Savannah and took her in his arms. He stroked the hair back from her hot face, damp with a million tears, and whispered in her ear, "It's all right. It's all right. You're free."

"F-free?" The word came out muffled against his shoulder. "My own mother. My own mother."

Connor's eyes locked with those of a woman heading into the office building, and her gait slowed.

"I'm going to get you in the car. Is that all right?"

Savannah nodded against his chest, and he tucked an arm around her waist and rose to his feet, half dragging her with him. He lowered her to the passenger seat and then lifted her legs inside.

When he was behind the wheel, he reached into the back of the car and plucked a handful of tissues from the box on the seat. "Here you go. You had me so scared."

She bunched up several and blew her nose. "Why would she do that, Connor?"

"To save her own skin. That shouldn't surprise you, Savannah. In fact, I don't know why I didn't think of it myself." He wedged a knuckle beneath her chin. "Georgie has always been about Georgie first…and you second. This doesn't mean your mother didn't love you. She did. That was clear to anyone who saw the two of you together. She just didn't know how to be the best mother. Her needs always came first. She was the same with my father. I know she loved Dad, too, but she loved herself more—always."

"I have to confront her." Savannah shredded the used tissues, creating a snowstorm in her lap. "I have to make sure she knows that I know the truth."

"Of course you do." He brushed the bits of paper from her lap. "But not now."

"Oh, my God. The meeting." She flipped down the visor and studied her puffy eyes and red nose in the mirror.

"Cancel it. Do it another day. You need time to process this."

"There's no way I'm going to cancel this meeting."

"Delay it a few hours. Get yourself together."

She aimed a grimace at the mirror. "Maybe I should go into the meeting looking like this. People will think I'm really broken up about Niles and figure I never could've killed him."

"Whatever you want, Savannah, but I think you need more time." He trailed his fingers down her arm. "It's still early. You can delay the meeting until later this afternoon. You want to go into Snap App looking like a million bucks. You're the CEO of the damned company now."

She sniffled and ran her fingers through her hair. Then she gasped, "Do you know what this means?"

"It means you didn't kill Manny...or anyone else."

She dug her fingernails into his thigh through the light wool of his slacks. "I didn't kill Manny, Connor. I mean, I still went along with Mom's story, which ended your father's life, but I didn't pull that trigger. I didn't black out because I'd murdered someone. I blacked out from the shock of knowing my mother had."

"My father was an adult, a police officer. He should've known better than you or your mother. He made the decision to take the blame and then paid the consequences."

"He would've done anything for Georgie."

Connor leaned over and kissed Savannah's damp cheek. "I can't blame him. That's the kind of love I can understand."

Her bottom lip trembled. "It's all so messed up."

"It's not messed up. It's all straightened out now." He started the engine. "And we're going to straighten out this other business, too."

"Not by going to the police." She put her hand on his arm. "I told you. I'm not putting you in that situation."

"We're getting close to the truth on our own. Maybe we can hand those homicide detectives a done deal, a solved case."

She gave him a watery smile. "If anyone

can do it, you can. I have faith in you, Connor Wells."

"I wish I'd had faith in you, Savannah."

"I gave you no reason to and you still had my back." She squared her shoulders. "I'm going to delay the meeting for two hours, have lunch with you and fix my face."

"Don't do anything to that face." He touched her cheek. "It doesn't need fixing. Nothing about you needs fixing."

She snorted, "Now you're just getting carried away."

A phone rang in the car and Connor reached for his on the console. "It's yours."

"If it's my mother, you're going to have to restrain me." She glanced at the display and her jaw tightened. "Unknown."

"If it's your blackmailer, you're going to have to restrain *me*."

She tapped the display and answered. "Hello?"

"Savannah?"

She'd put her phone on speaker, and the man's voice filled the car.

"Yes. Who is this?"

"Brian Donahue."

She jerked her head toward Connor. "Did you kill Niles?"

"No! And neither did you."

"Damn straight. Who said I did and where are you?"

"I know what's going on, and I can fill you in if you meet me tonight."

"Tell me now, over the phone."

"Can you be sure your cell isn't bugged?"

Savannah held the phone in front of her face and studied it, as if seeing it for the first time. "No."

"Give me another number to use and I'll text the time and location."

"Not the same place where I met Letty."

Donahue made a strangled noise. "You met Letty?"

"You're trying to tell me you didn't know about that meeting?"

"Savannah, Letty's dead."

"I know that." Savannah jabbed Connor

in the shoulder. "But how do you unless you were there?"

"Where have you been? It's on the news."

Savannah gasped, "What do you know about Letty?"

"Nothing. Give me the number and I'll text you the meeting info."

Connor held up his phone and tapped it.

Savannah reeled off Connor's cell number and ended the call. Seconds later a time and location for the meeting came through on Connor's phone.

Savannah put her hands together as if in prayer, holding her phone between them. "They found Letty."

"I'm glad they did, aren't you?"

"Yes, but it makes that photo of me with her body a stick of dynamite now."

"It always was, but I think it's just insurance to use in case you get too close to the truth." He pulled the car into a grocery store parking lot.

"I thought we were getting lunch before the meeting."

"We are." He parked the car. "Here. We'll pick up a few things and head to the beach, have lunch there and relax."

She plucked at her navy slacks. "Dressed in office clothes? Even you're dressed up."

"We'll be careful."

She took his hand. "Thanks for putting my mom's betrayal into perspective for me."

"You're not a killer, Savannah—self-defense or otherwise. But I'm not letting you off the hook."

Her cheeks flushed. "You're not?"

"You're going back to see Thomas. You need a professional to help you process this. I'm just a bandage."

She pressed a kiss against his palm and folded his hand over it. "Best damned bandage I've ever had in my life."

CONNOR WAS RIGHT—as usual. The lunch, the beach and just being together all helped to set her spinning world back on its axis. But Savannah still felt a hole in her stomach—a hole where her mother's love should've been.

But she had work to do and that bandage had to do its job for now.

Later that afternoon, Connor pulled into an executive parking space beneath her building. "Are you sure you want me to go in with you?"

"I'd like to show you the office—what I helped build—even if it *is* all going to turn to ashes before my eyes."

"If anyone can repair the damage, you can."

"With the help of my CFO, Nick. He's the money guy." She slid from the car and shook out her jacket before putting it on.

Connor opened the glass door that led from the parking structure to the offices of Snap App.

Kelly, the receptionist, squealed and scooted around the desk. She threw her arms around Savannah. "Welcome back, Savannah. We're all so happy you're back in charge…but of course, devastated by Niles's murder."

"Of course. It's been horrible."

Kelly put a hand to her throat. "Do you think his housekeeper had anything to do with it? She committed suicide."

"I have no idea. I'll let the detectives figure things out." She patted Kelly on the back. "I'm here to figure things out for Snap App."

She and Connor took the elevator up to the seventh floor. When the doors opened, she said, "My office is up here, but the big conference room is on the first floor. We'll be having the meeting there, but first I'm going to have my chat with Dee Dee."

"Nice digs." Connor turned in a circle, taking in the glass-walled offices with their views of the marina and downtown.

"Savannah." Nick Fresco emerged from his office, straightening his impeccable tie, and took her hands in his long, bony fingers. "It's good to see you back. This company needs you."

"Needs something right now. I just hope I have the right words to say."

"You will." He squeezed her hands and

then glanced at Connor, his dark eyes jumping to the curls at his hairline.

"This is Connor Wells. Connor, my trusty CFO, Nick Fresco."

"Nice to meet you, Connor." As he shook Connor's hand he stooped slightly, a habit he'd likely developed from being six foot six. "New employee?"

"No, I'm just her chauffeur."

Savannah poked Connor's arm.

Connor tilted back his head. "Basketball player?"

"I've shot some hoops in my day."

She tugged on Connor's sleeve. "Do you want to see my office? I haven't occupied it for a while, but I kept it intact."

Dee Dee peered out of another office. "Hey, Savannah. Are we still meeting before the meeting?"

Savannah swallowed and curved her stiff lips into a smile. "Yeah, I was just going to show Connor my office."

Dee Dee stepped into the corridor and

flipped her dark hair over her shoulders. "Oh, this is the famous Connor Wells."

Savannah introduced them and then showed Connor her corner office.

"I'm impressed." He wandered to the window with his hands in his pockets and gazed at the view. "Are you going to be working here?"

She came up behind him and wrapped her arms around his waist. "I can do my work anywhere...even on a vineyard."

His back stiffened and she held her breath. Had she gone too far, too fast?

He turned and smoothed a lock of her hair from her forehead. "Can I look around while you're with Dee Dee? I'll show myself out when I'm done and do a little work at that coffeehouse down the block while you finish with your other meetings."

"Sounds good. I'll text you when I'm finished for the day...or night, and then we can eat if we have time before that meeting with Brian."

"We're still on for later?"

Nick's voice startled her and she spun around, jerking her hair out of Connor's fingers. "Yes, we have a lot to go over."

Nick rapped his knuckles on the door frame. "I'm going to go down to the conference room and make sure everything's set up for the meeting. Nice to meet you, Connor."

Connor held up his hand.

As soon as Nick left, Dee Dee took his place at the door. "Ready?"

"I am." Savannah flicked her fingers toward the door. "Make yourself at home, Connor. I'll text you when I'm ready to leave, and then I'll meet you downstairs at my parking space."

"Good luck." He shut the door behind him.

Savannah took a deep breath and perched on the edge of a love seat against one wall. "Have a seat, Dee."

Dee Dee pulled a chair across from Savannah and sank into it. "What a crazy week. You heard about Letty, right?"

"I did."

"Do you think she killed Niles? Was blackmailing him or something and then took her own life?"

"I don't know. That doesn't sound like Letty, but then I guess you never know about people, do you?"

Dee Dee cocked her head. "I guess not."

"Dee—" Savannah pulled a folder from her briefcase "—can you tell me why Niles made a lump sum payment to you that he was trying to hide?"

Dee Dee's face dropped and she clutched the arms of the chair. "What do you mean?"

Savannah whipped out the sheet of paper. "It's here in black and white, Dee Dee. What happened?"

"Are you going to tell the cops?" She pressed her hand against her heart. "I swear I didn't have anything to do with Niles's murder."

"What's the payment for?"

"Sexual harassment."

Savannah's mouth dropped open. "Niles harassed you?"

"We had a brief affair, Savannah." Dee Dee dropped her head.

"While he was still married to me?"

"Yes. I'm sorry."

"It was consensual and mutual?"

"Aside from Niles being my boss, it was. I am sorry."

"And then you threatened to sue him?"

"He was so arrogant, Savannah. You know that."

"But he took money from the company to pay you. Did *you* know *that*?" Savannah smacked the file on her knee. "You should've just sued him for sexual harassment and settled with the insurance company."

"I—I didn't want my husband to find out. It would've killed Victor."

"Give me one good reason why I shouldn't tell those homicide detectives."

"I protected you, Savannah." Dee Dee pushed up from the chair. "We all did. You don't think you're their prime suspect? You are. We could all tell that, and we tried our best to steer them away from you."

"I didn't do it." Savannah shouted the words, with more confidence than ever. She hadn't killed Manny. Someone had drugged her the night of Niles's murder. She was no killer.

"Neither did I." Dee Dee leaned against the window. "I was home with Victor. The police already checked my alibi."

"Mine, too."

"Then neither of us has anything to worry about."

She wouldn't go that far.

Dee Dee turned, clutching her hands in front of her. "And you have no reason to tell the police about my agreement with Niles, right? It has nothing to do with anything."

"I wouldn't say that, Dee Dee. As I mentioned before, you never really know anyone, do you? You're fired."

"Savannah. Is it because of the affair? It didn't mean anything, and you were so over Niles by then." She tipped her head toward the window, where Connor had appeared. "Because of him, right?"

Connor raised a pen and pointed toward the exit.

Nodding, Savannah waved at him. Then she turned back to Dee Dee. "It's about trust, Dee. I'm sick of being betrayed by people I thought I could trust." Savannah stood up and brushed off her slacks. "The good news? You don't have to go to the meeting."

Savannah walked out of her office and looked around the empty floor. Everyone must be at the meeting…waiting for her. Time for her to start acting like a CEO, and she'd just taken her first step.

When she walked into the conference room, it erupted in applause and then everyone stood up. Savannah crossed her hands over her chest. Maybe you never really knew anyone, but this felt good.

Nick ushered her to the front of the room with a grin. "Snap App's founder and our new CEO, Savannah Martell."

The applause swelled again, and Savannah strode to the podium to take her place in front of her employees.

For the next hour, she stuck to her script. She praised Niles, although the words stuck in her throat, and she put forth a plan going forward. She didn't mention the funny business with the accounting, but she planned to address it with Nick.

The meeting seemed to fly by, but by the time she finished it was past quitting time for everyone, and then it got even later as half the company approached her to say hello, shake hands and even drop a few weird hints about Niles.

Finally, the room cleared, until she faced Nick, alone.

"Whew." She dropped into the nearest chair. "How'd I do?"

"Great. Didn't you see the reaction of the troops?" He crossed one long leg over the other.

Savannah patted her chest. "It warmed my heart. Should we get down to business? I have the papers I want to discuss with you in my briefcase."

Nick pointed at the ceiling. "And I have

mine upstairs. Let's have this discussion in my office. I have a surprise for you."

"I don't need any surprises, Nick." She tilted her head to one side. Nick was usually by the book. That was what she liked about him.

"Okay, no surprises." He held up his hands. "I bought a nice bottle of champagne to celebrate your homecoming. Just a sip or two."

"Actually, I could use a sip or two. I've had a rough day—rough week."

"I'll take this for you." He grabbed her briefcase and hitched it over his shoulder.

As they rode up the elevator together, she broke the news about Dee Dee.

Nick's eyes popped out of their sockets. "Dee and Niles? That fool. I'm sorry, Savannah, but the man had no discipline."

"Tell me about it."

When they reached the executive floor, Nick ushered her into his office. He reached into the minifridge on the floor beside his desk, withdrew a magnum of champagne and hoisted it in the air. "The good stuff."

He took a couple glasses from a credenza. "Do you mind if they're not crystal flutes?"

"You're mistaking me for Niles."

"Never." He popped the cork and splashed a quantity of the sparkling liquid in each glass, where it foamed and bubbled. He raised his glass to her. "To a new era at Snap App."

"A new era." She clinked her glass against his and took a sip. Then she reached into her briefcase and pulled out the file with the misrepresentations. "And it's going to start right here."

Smoothing out the papers on the table in front of them, she launched into a description of what Niles had been doing with the orders.

She didn't have to explain much to Nick. He was their finance guy. He'd know all about the practice of accelerating revenues.

"There's more, Nick." She took another gulp of champagne, her long discourse making her thirsty. "I think Brian Donahue may have known something about this."

"Brian?" He rolled his glass between his hands. "He's missing."

"Not anymore. I—I'm meeting him tonight. He contacted me and told me he had info about Niles."

"That's not safe, Savannah." Nick tipped more of the shimmering liquid into her glass. "That guy's a loose cannon."

"I'll be taking Connor with me. He'll keep me safe." She yawned and tapped the file. "But what are we going to do about this mess, Nick?"

"I'll take care of it, Savannah." He scooped up the papers and shoved them back into the folder. Then he tossed it onto his desk.

She wrinkled her nose and yawned again. "What are you doing?"

"I'm gonna bury that information so deep it'll never surface."

Savannah's head buzzed and she tried to work up some outrage, but she was too tired. Her gaze tracked to the champagne still fizzing in her glass. As she reached for it again, she knocked it over with one flailing hand.

She struggled to hold on to consciousness, but felt it slipping away. She was going to black out again…but this time the dead body in the room would be hers.

Chapter Eighteen

Connor checked his phone again for what seemed like the hundredth time. The meetings must be going well. Maybe Fresco, Savannah's CFO, would be able to help right the Snap App ship.

He shoved back from his laptop and stretched. Even though they'd had that late lunch, he'd be ready for dinner before their meeting with Brian and the drive back to San Juan Beach.

He swirled the dregs of the coffee left in his cup and then set it down. He'd head over and wait for her in the parking lot. He didn't much trust this Brian character she was meeting later.

His cell phone buzzed and he checked the display. He read the text from Savannah with a groan, and then eyed the refrigerated display case next to the register.

Savannah had decided to go out with Dee Dee for a drink before the meeting with Brian, and had asked him to pick her up at the bar in another two hours. His stomach rumbled.

He didn't think it was a great idea for her to drink before seeing Brian, but she'd had a rough day—and he'd have her back. He responded to her text with a thumbs-up emoji and ordered himself a bagel and cream cheese.

As he sat down with the warm bagel, the woman at the next table smiled at him. "Do you have a pen I can borrow? Mine just ran out of ink."

He felt in his front pocket for the pen he'd grabbed from Nick Fresco's desk on his way out of the Snap App offices and plucked it from his pocket. "Here you go."

"Thanks. I just need it for a minute." She took it from him and flipped open a notebook.

Connor scooped out some cream cheese and spread it on one half of his bagel. He crunched into the bagel and pulled his laptop close to finish reviewing the report from his chemist on the winery.

The woman stretched across the space between their tables and tapped the pen on the surface before dropping it. "Thank you."

The pen rolled off the table and fell to the floor, where a piece broke off.

"I'm so sorry. Was it an expensive pen?"

Connor leaned to the side to retrieve it. As he picked it up, a feather of fear brushed the back of his neck. Where had he seen this particular type of pen before?

His heart slammed against his chest and he almost tipped out of the chair. He dropped the pen to the floor himself and scrambled out of his seat. Under the woman's wide eyes, he brought the heel of his shoe down on the object, splintering it into pieces.

"Wh-what's wrong? I'll replace the pen if you like."

He pinched the pieces in a napkin and plopped back in his chair. Hunching over the table, he stirred through the bits of plastic, his chest slamming against his rib cage.

The pen he'd taken from Nick Fresco's desk was a spy pen. The same type Savannah had been carrying around in her purse for a few days. The type someone had slipped into her purse the night Savannah was drugged and Niles was murdered. The same kind that had broken in just this way that day in Niles's office.

And Savannah and Nick had a meeting tonight together, alone.

His heart galloping, Connor pulled into the empty parking structure. Everyone had left. The meeting was over.

Savannah had given him her location badge to get in and out of the building, and he used it now to gain access to the reception area. Some small voice in his ear kept him from charging up seven flights of stairs yelling Savannah's name.

He eased open the door to the stairwell and glided up the steps barely breaking a sweat, his pumping adrenaline giving him the strength of ten men. He'd need it—that and his gun. He patted the weapon in his waistband he'd brought for the meeting with Brian.

When he reached the seventh floor, he held his breath and pushed down the door handle. He gave the door a little shove and stopped, peering through the crack. The stairwell was down the hall from the main offices and he could see the only lunchroom from his vantage point.

He opened the door wide enough to slip through, and then closed it on a whisper. He crept toward the offices and paused when he heard voices, male and female. Shutting his eyes, he blew out a breath. He'd recognize Savannah's voice anywhere.

If she and Fresco were still meeting, Connor would get her out of here, and then they could compile the evidence against Fresco without the CFO even knowing they were onto him.

The voices became clearer, and still, Connor held back, inching his way toward a cubicle across from the offices. He flattened himself against one wall of the cubicle and waited until he could hear the voices again.

Savannah's voice, low and slightly slurred, came from the office—her office. "This is not going to work, Nick."

"Of course it is. You murdered your husband to get your hands on the company, his life insurance, the house—take your pick. Then you killed Letty because she was going to blackmail you with the button. I have proof of that."

"That's not proof. And I have the knife, remember?"

Nick laughed, "I should've realized you'd be a formidable foe, Savannah. Niles was easy. That button will be good enough. And when the cops find your dead body here at the office, they'll assume you were filled with remorse and hanged yourself."

His words hit Connor on the back of the head like a sledgehammer. His muscles coiled, ready to pounce. But pounce on what? He couldn't see into the office. He didn't want to push Fresco into doing anything yet.

"I have…whatever you drugged me with… in my body. The autopsy report will show that."

"So what? You needed to take something before the act to steady your nerves…just like you drugged Niles to make stabbing him easier."

"I don't understand why you're doing this, Nick. You were never even on my radar. I had no idea you and Niles were cooking the books together. The paperwork doesn't implicate you."

"It was my plan from the start—kill Niles and frame you. Your meeting with Brian tonight just accelerated the timeline."

"Brian knows, doesn't he? That's why you

fired him. He was going to tell me every-thing tonight."

Fresco snorted, "I wouldn't count on that. He's all over the place, but I can handle Brian—I've done it before."

Savannah coughed. "Why didn't you just kill both of us that night?"

"And leave the cops searching for a sus-pect? No, thanks."

The sound of a dragging chair had Connor dropping to his hands and knees and mak-ing a move out of the cubicle. He had to see what was going on. Had to determine a way to stop this madness.

"Connor is coming back here to pick me up any minute. This is not going to work, Nick. We can make a deal. I'll work with you."

Savannah's speech had lost its drowsy edge and contained a hint of desperation.

Connor clenched his hands into fists, curs-ing the modern glass walls of these offices. The minute he popped up, Fresco would spot him.

"I took care of Connor, too."

"What?" Savannah choked.

"Oh, not like that, but if he doesn't stop snooping around, I will take extreme measures." Fresco clicked his tongue. "I meant I sent him a text from you toward the end of the all-hands meeting, letting him know you'd be going out for drinks with Dee Dee. He doesn't even know you're still here. He'll be waiting for you at some bar downtown in about an hour. And like you said—you two never suspected me. Did you really think that nitwit Tiffany could've pulled this off, or even her psychotic boyfriend? Letty? Come on."

"I won't tell anyone, Nick. You can resign from the company with a fat bonus and I'll fix everything."

Fresco laughed, "I don't believe that for a second. You were always the moral partner. Niles was the dirtbag. That's how I knew he'd be up for a little financial maneuvering."

"Stop this."

Was that a plea to him? Connor couldn't stand to listen to any more of this.

Clutching the gun in his hands, he rose slowly from the floor to face the windows of Savannah's office. Rage boiled his blood and seared his skin when he saw Fresco slipping a noose around Savannah's neck as she stood on a chair.

Fresco spun around, one hand on Savannah's back, the other on the rope encircling her throat.

Connor growled, "Let her go."

"Are you sure about that?" Fresco tapped the leg of the chair with the toe of his wingtip. "One solid kick and she swings."

"One shot and you're dead." Connor took aim at Fresco's head.

"I'm not going down alone, Wells. She'll come with me. And then you'll have quite a bit of explaining to do—maybe starting with how you impeded a murder investigation by lying about the prime suspect's whereabouts." Fresco moved closer to the chair. "I have to admit Savannah impressed me with her criminal know-how. I thought the cops would be arresting her right away once they pinged her cell phone, and found that knife. If I were you, I'd be a little worried about being with a woman who knows how to cover her tracks as effortlessly as Savannah does. Lots of practice there."

Connor's jaw hardened. He could take the head shot and maybe Fresco wouldn't have time to kick that chair out from under Savannah. Or maybe he would have time, but Connor could rush across the room and grab her before she hanged.

He stared hard into Fresco's eyes, his finger tightening on the trigger.

A split second later, Savannah hoisted her feet from the chair and slammed them into Fresco's ribs.

The man staggered to the side and then lunged for Savannah's legs, which were bicycling in the air.

That was his girl, and nobody was going to hurt his girl ever again.

Connor took the shot.

Epilogue

Savannah stretched out in the hammock and curled her toes. She held up her wineglass to the setting sun. "Yours is going to be better than this, isn't it?"

Connor, on the other side of the hammock, facing her, took a sip of wine and swirled it around in his mouth. "Damn right."

"You'll have to send some to the detectives when it's ready. Detective Paulson called me this morning and told me they were wrapping up the case against Nick Fresco."

"I'm not sure Paulson ever did believe you weren't at the house that night."

"Maybe not." She trailed a hand over the edge of the hammock through the tall, cool grass. "But when they found the murder weapon with both Niles's and Nick's blood on it, that sealed the deal for them, and Brian Donahue's statement helped."

"Told you A.J. was a pro."

She slid her sunglasses down to the tip of her nose. "I don't know why Nick would keep the murder weapon with his own blood on it."

"He didn't keep it. He planted it on you and figured you'd dispose of it. Probably didn't realize his blood was on the knife, but knew yours was because that's what he used to cut you. Didn't remember that you were left-handed, though." Connor grabbed her bare foot and ran his knuckle down her arch. "That was a stroke of luck when I grabbed that pen from Fresco's desk. I can't believe he'd leave something like that out in plain sight, but then he probably figured he could plant another one on you when you were in the office. Did he ever explain why he made his move that night, when you didn't even suspect him?"

"He always planned to stage my suicide." She shivered despite the warm sun beating down on her legs. "But when I stupidly told him I was meeting Brian, he snapped. He thought Brian might've decided to tell me that he discovered the anomalies in the finances and had been paid off to keep quiet."

"Who knows if that's what Brian was going to do?"

"I still don't know. He won't return my calls." She pinged the side of her glass with her fingernail. "But my mom finally did."

Connor sat up and the hammock swayed from side to side. "Georgie called you back? Did you confront her?"

"I did."

"I'm sure she had excuses for what she did."

"Of course. She told me in all seriousness that the cops would've gone easier on a young woman who'd been fighting off Manny's advances than an older woman who stood to get her hands on Manny's assets." Savannah

swiped the back of her hand across her stinging nose. "But she told me she loved me."

"She ain't the only one." Connor chafed
her foot between his hands.

She tossed the rest of her wine overboard
and placed the glass on the ground. "You're
too far away."

Connor held out his arms, and she scrambled across the swinging hammock and
landed on his chest, tucking her head against
his shoulder. "I thought of a good name for
the winery."

"Really?" He stroked her hair and kissed
the top of her head. "Let me guess… Savannah's?"

"Nope. Alibi Vineyards."

Connor wrapped his arms around her, and
they laughed so hard the hammock flipped
over and dumped them on the ground.

"Be careful. You're going to have Detective Paulson knocking on your door again."

"Let him come at me. Let 'em all come at
me." Resting her head against his chest, she

ran her fingers through his long hair. "If you believe in me, I can face anything."

"Oh, I believe in you, Savannah Martell…"

Her head jerked up and she met his blue eyes. Had he almost said *for now*?

Then he took her face in his hands and kissed her…and she didn't even care.

* * * * *

LET'S TALK
Romance

For exclusive extracts, competitions
and special offers, find us online:

f facebook.com/millsandboon

⊙ @millsandboonuk

🐦 @millsandboon

Or get in touch on 0844 844 1351*

For all the latest titles coming soon,
visit millsandboon.co.uk/nextmonth